Truth or Dare

Michelle Ventura

Michelle Ventura

Dare to live your truth romance

TITLE TRUTH OR DARE

Copyright ©2019 by Michelle Ventura

ISBN-13: 978-1-7350868-0-4

This book is a work of fiction. Any references to historical events real people or real places are used fictitiously. Names, characters, places, and events are products of the authors imagination and any resemblance to actual events or places or persons, living or dead, is entirely coincidental.

Third Edition: June 2021

Cover design by Michelle Ventura and Robert Johnson
Editing and author services by Debbe Johnson, OTP Author Services

To Elizabeth Snow-Richmond, for teaching me what true friendship is. Even through the silence and distance, we have remained forever strong.

Acknowledgments

So many people played a part in the writing and completion of this book, I can't possibly thank them all here. I have spent so many years writing that the people involved in my growth as a writer, the cheerleaders, and the critics, all of whom helped me immensely are too many to list and sadly, I've lost track of some of them.

Barbara Smith, I thank you for the many hours of critique, editing and character feedback. Your insight has made me a better writer.

To Deanna Sybrant, my sister and friend and her husband Joe for your support with the techy stuff I so hate.

Kat Brown, my dear friend and Stephani Fuller for being my Beta readers and to Terry Wells-Brown, a fellow writer and published author for your help in making my lifelong dream come true.

To my family for their love and support and for cheering me on.

And finally, to my son Jack Overton who has taught me the true meaning of unconditional love. Being a parent is by the far the hardest job and the greatest joy. I am so very proud to call you my son.

Chapter One

Riley Snow lifted her glass of Rombauer Chardonnay. She and Beth, her best friend since grade school clinked glasses.

The smile that split Riley's face brightened the trendy, black and chrome lounge in which they sat, sharing Bruschetta, a Caesar Salad and a bottle of delicious wine. "To my freedom! And fortune!" Riley took a sip of the smooth buttery wine, savoring the flavor. She had enjoyed Rombauer twice. Now she could afford it every day, if she drank daily - which she didn't. But if she did. She could even afford Silver Oak she once heard referred to as 'liquid sex'. "The rat bastard took so long to sign the separation papers, he had to give me half of his lottery winnings."

When Riley's lawyer suggested she go after half of her cheating ex-husband's winnings, she had hesitated. Riley wanted the break quick and simple, but true to his slimy form, Robert decided to fight dirty. He expected to keep the house and everything in it even though his cheating ways were the reason she'd left. So, Riley took half the money, gave him the house with everything in it and walked straight to an investment company to deposit her check.

Now she could chase after her lifelong dream.

A dark scowl crossed her friend's face. "Robert's an ass. He deserved to lose every dime just for being an insensitive, self-centered, egotistical prick who can't keep his dick in his pants." Beth waved her hand in the air, "You're better off without that selfish bastard. Now you can focus on writing your book, which you probably would've published already if you'd never married the prick." Beth took a long sip of wine. "It's time to have a little fun. Find a man who will appreciate you for the beautiful woman you are and treat you like a queen."

Riley played with the stem of her wine glass. "Wouldn't that be nice."

Robert had been her high-school crush. Later in college they'd reconnected while she was working toward her degree and fallen in love with him all over again. He'd treated her like nothing more than a convenience. She just hadn't seen it.

After five years of marriage, she had come home early to find his bare ass bouncing in their bed with an 18-year- old-wanna-be actress from LA. Riley had packed a suitcase and moved to Lake Tahoe without a backward glance. Well, that wasn't entirely true. She fought hard to accept that Robert's betrayal wasn't about her. Sometimes she won the fight, but she hadn't fully won the war. Even as a child she struggled with her self-esteem. Having a brother who always chastised her for her weight or her looks made her feel less than good enough. She had never had a boyfriend in high school like all of her friends which only reinforced her negative self-image issues.

Beth snapped her fingers in front of Riley's face. "You're going way too serious on me. Let's do something crazy." Beth leaned in closer, "Let's play truth or dare."

Riley laughed. "What's the point in that? You know everything there is to know about me."

"Okay, then I dare you to hit on that Hottie," Beth pointed across the room.

Riley locked in on a big hulk of a man sitting at the bar. His faded blue t-shirt spread across a broad chest, thick, deeply tanned triceps and, oh that Six-pack...

Riley picked up the Rombauer and topped off her glass then poured the rest into Beth's. "Much as I'd like a night of hot steamy sex with a hard body like that one over there," Riley tilted her head toward Six-pack, "I've resigned myself to the idea of mediocrity," Riley pointed to a middle aged man at a table by the window, "with the likes of him."

Her sexual encounters were few; most of her experience from her less than stellar sex life with Robert. From the books she read, for research of course, she knew sex could be way more fun than anything she'd experienced and though she fantasized about doing it with someone like Six-pack, she really didn't think she could handle him.

Beth sighed. "Oh, come on, Riley. Don't let Robert's insecurity in himself take that from you. He craved sex. He was a, umm, what's it called? Nymphomaniac?"

"No. Silly. That's the female sex maniac. The male version is a Satyriasis."

"Yeah. Whatever." Beth took a long sip of her wine and set the glass down. "The point is, Robert's affair had nothing to do with you." She reached across the table and lifted Riley's chin, looking her in the eye. "You couldn't save him. He gave you nothing but expected everything from you, including turning a blind eye to his behavior and when you wouldn't play, he took his marbles elsewhere. I say good riddance. You are so better off without him."

Riley swiped at the moisture in her eyes. Beth had been her best friend since forever, she always had her back. And even though they had fought over boys - Beth always won - Riley loved her like a sister. "Thanks for the vote of confidence, but let's get off this subject and go back to our celebration." Riley swallowed back her tears. "Screw Robert and his little bimbo bitch."

"That's the spirit," Beth said. "Let's get another bottle and plot our strategies for how you're going to take Six-pack home."

Beth flagged the waiter and pointed to the empty bottle.

Riley laughed, her eyes roaming over the hunky man cut right from the pages of every woman's fantasy magazine. "I bet he's a total player and probably doesn't do vanilla." Riley giggled as Beth choked on her wine.

"Where the hell did that come from?"

Riley shrugged. Beth was the daring one, the friendly one, and the beautiful one. She had always gotten the boys. Riley had been overweight and shy as a teenager. She'd only slimmed down when she started college because she'd joined the rowing team. She managed to drop from a size fourteen to a ten, but struggled daily to keep off the weight. "You know I'd never to be able to hold my own with someone like that. Look at him? He's fucking hot and probably rich. He'd have no interest in me."

The waiter arrived with their wine and poured them each a glass. They thanked him and he scurried off.

Beth turned her attention back to Riley and smiled, shaking her head. She reached over and grasped Riley's hand. "Riley, you have got to get over this low self-image thing you have going on. You are beautiful and smart and have the world at your fingertips. Sit back and enjoy the ride. You'd be surprised at the possibilities if you just open yourself up to them."

Riley fought back tears. Beth was right. She needed to let go of the past and let the future unfold. She leaned back in her chair and glanced over at McHottie. *Damn, but he is HOT!* Maybe he'd teach her a thing or two about what real intense hot and heavy gotta-have-you-now sex is like. As if she had the ovaries to go after a man like him. But the very idea of it made her tingle with anticipation. It must be the wine.

"Come on, Riley. We're going to say hi." Beth topped off their wine and stood.

4

Riley followed Beth to the bar, her Chardonnay sloshing in the glass. The crowd had thinned, but the closest bar stool was three away from Six-pack. Close up, he was even more stunning than Riley could've conjured up in her most erotic fantasy.

His eyes were a misty green, shadowed by heavy dark lashes. Black hair begged to have fingers running through it dripped down to shoulders thick and taut. His biceps bulged under the tight sleeves of his t-shirt.

He could make you wet just by looking at you.

And then his perusal settled on Riley.

"He's checking you out," Beth nudged Riley in side. "I dare you to go for it."

Riley smiled, her stomach flipped and she felt heat moving deep into her face and body. *Oh no. I am so not ready for this game of cat and mouse.* Riley shifted on the stool without taking her eyes off of Six-pack. All the while a fluttering sensation caused her to quiver in all the wrong -- right places. She crossed her legs and squeezed tight.

"He's smiling at me, what do I do?" The heat continued to build as he gave her the proverbial once over.

Beth giggled. "Just go with it, silly girl."

Riley regretted having worn the see-through white lace blouse with the slinky white satin bra beneath. Her breasts went taught at his scrutiny and she had to squeeze her legs together to stop the flitting sensations that continued to dart through her center. His eyes met hers and she shivered at the raw lust she saw in the darkening green depths. God, he was testosterone dynamite and her fuse burned dangerously close to explosion. Her panties already damp with desire. She wasn't up for taking on a man like Six-pack. Was she?

She and Robert had a decent sex life. She didn't consider herself an expert, and probably wasn't very daring in the bedroom but they had

had sex a couple of times a week and he always said he'd enjoyed it. But he cheated on her, so maybe she really wasn't all that much fun in bed.

Riley turned back to Beth who hailed the bartender and asked him to pour one for Six-pack. She was ready to chicken out and run from the room when a young blonde with big breasts sidled up to the hunk.

"Shit," Beth muttered. "Cancel that," she said to the bartender. "Let's go to *Altitude* and dance," Beth didn't wait for a reply. She grabbed Riley's hand and dragged her through the lounge.

Riley glanced back to see that the hunky guy was in serious conversation with the blonde. *Doesn't that just figure? The SOB is just like Robert. They're all pigs!*

Riley pasted on a smile and waved to him as she left the lounge. *Prick, bastard.* She crossed the atrium lobby of the Luxury Suites, flushed with embarrassment, disappointment and sexual excitement.

She'd never been promiscuous. She hadn't even really dated all that much. Growing up overweight with a bunch of rich snobs kept her self-esteem in the far recesses of Hades all through her teenage years. When she went to college, she focused on her studies, never attending frat parties or hanging out at the popular party joints. She probably dated three or four guys, all very nerdy and focused. She'd slept with one of them, losing her virginity and regretting it when he promptly dumped her.

Then she'd run into Robert, her high school crush. He'd charmed her into bed and been so attentive sexually that she never noticed how inattentive he was with her feelings or interests. They always hung out with his friends. Did the things he wanted to do. Saw the movies he wanted to see.

Even then it was always all about him. Why hadn't she seen it?

She was naïve and inexperienced and clearly had bad taste in men. But she had to admit that Six-pack incited responses she had never had before.

But sex wasn't all there was to a relationship. Trust and loyalty were far more important. She wanted a marriage built on trust and friendship. A man with a sense of humor and a sense of honor. Babies and a dog. A house with a white picket fence. Every girls' dream. And if the sex was good, she'd be a content woman.

Beth opened the door leading outside and the cold February wind snatched Riley from her reverie. She pulled her leather jacket closed and ducked against the biting wind, following Beth across and down the street toward the Casino that boasted the best dance club in town.

The Lake Tahoe streets were filled with the confusion of President's weekend tourists. The snow that threatened had yet to fall, so traipsing across the crowded blacktop in her stiletto boots and bottle of wine buzz wasn't a problem for her.

She sighed when they entered the jingling hustle and bustle of the Casino. As she moved deeper into the depths of desperation and smoke, she pictured the look in those sexy green eyes.

If only she could do the meaningless one-night stand. Certainly, someone like Mr. McHottie Six-pack would be a candidate for wild and crazy sex. The kind she'd read about in the many romance novels she'd read over the years. She shivered, the sexual attraction and desire still zinging through her veins from Six-packs intense stare.

Chapter Two

S hane Blackstone was normally a very patient man. He'd gone straight from high school into the Navy. He worked hard for what he wanted. When he turned twelve, he decided he wanted to be a Navy SEAL. Four years after joining the Navy he entered the BUDS program but had to ring out when he was injured in a training exercise.

He'd left the Navy and went to college where he earned his Master's Degree in Criminology. Then he joined the DEA.

His whole life had been about planning and the one thing he excelled at was patience. Except when it came to his little sister. Her mood swings and crazy behavior were enough to make Shane batty in the head. That she had a good reason for her sporadic behavior didn't make it any easier, but it helped Shane reach deep for a little extra of that well-honed patience.

He'd had to take a deep breath and count to ten when she strolled into the bar. But that was only half his problem now. The hot redhead he had been following thought Katie his date.

As if.

The way his dick hardened when Red's nipples responded to his hungry stare...

Stop it, Shane. You have a job to do. She's your only lead.

He set Katie on his stool and followed the redhead through the lobby, watching as she crossed the street and dashed into Harrah's. Good. He'd find her after he packed Katie into Nick's car.

He stormed back through the lobby and into the lounge, with Katie in his sights.

Shane knew Katie was still reeling from their parents' death. Her behavior went from catatonic to extreme without warning. The problem was that Katie didn't remember what had happened. Some days she would drink until she passed out, or score weed from her old high school friends and smoke until she couldn't move. Even though her memory of the night their parents died remained locked in her subconscious, she behaved as though she were trying to forget.

"Why did you make Nick bring you here?" Shane asked in the lowest voice he could manage.

"I'm tired of sitting at home. I need to get out of that place and you keep leaving me."

"You can't be at a bar, Katie. You aren't old enough." He grabbed her purse from the counter top with one hand and her wrist with the other.

"Then let's sit at a table. I'm hungry." Katie tried to pull away.

"You're going with Nick. If he wants to stop and get some food, that's fine. But it's time to go."

Katie dug in her heels and snatched her hand away, sliding into a nearby booth.

Shane took a deep breath, followed her and sat down. "I know this is a tough time for you, but I'm on an assignment and I need to get back to work. Now, Katie." Shane's tone left no room for argument. Katie looked up at him, then around the bright bar. Finally, she nodded and stood. Shane pulled her through the lobby and into the space between the inner and outer doors.

"Who the hell do you think you are?" Katie hissed pounding at his chest when he released her. "You are NOT my father. You can't come back after leaving me to deal with Mom and Dad's death - five months late, and tell me what to do you bastard!" The venom in Katie's voice pierced his heart. "I had to bury them. Alone. Who the hell are you to order me around?"

Shane pulled her close, held her tightly to his body while she shook with rage and then with violent sobs. "I'm sorry, Katiedid." He ran his hand over her back. "I tried to get back sooner. I really did. I'm so sorry." The gnawing guilt consumed him, bringing moisture to his eyes. He slammed his lids closed to stave off the tears.

When she calmed, Shane let her go. He knew he should go home with her, but his well-honed gut told him that he needed to catch up with the redhead. Actually, her hair was more brown than red, but when the lights hit her shoulder length hair just so, the red glistened like snow on a bough in the moonlight. Shane was pulled to her like a magnet to a steel pole.

Just one look at her and his pole turned to steel.

"I promise I'll be home soon, Katie. I just need to take care of something. Please, grab food and go home, I'll see you in an hour or two."

Katie crossed her arms over her over-exposed chest. "What's so important?"

Being DEA meant deep cover so he'd told Katie he was taking over the gym their father had owned, which was basically true. He did run the gym, for now. It was a good front for taking down the people who killed Shane and Katie's parents.

He walked outside and searched for Nick's car. "Shane, please let me go with you." He tucked her into the passenger seat when Nick came to a stop.

"I'll be home soon."

He closed the door on Katie's protestations. She was hard-headed but she was his only family. Shane loved her and would do whatever it took to take care of her.

He had failed to take care of his parents. He had failed to take care of his partner during the investigation of the largest drug cartel in Florida. His cover there had been so deep he hadn't been able to get home for his own parents' funeral. He had failed on so many levels, but he wouldn't fail to protect his sister. Ever.

He would die first.

Pulling his cell phone from his pocket, Shane punched in his best friend and new partner's's number.

Nick answered on the first ring.

"Take her for some food, Nick."

"No problem." Nick pulled into traffic.

Shane waved. "Thanks."

Nick had been watching over Katie since Shane learned his parents had been murdered. Recruited while still in college for his scary skills, Nick went straight into the DEA as a computer analyst. They'd sent him to Quantico where he'd become a trained assassin. His position had slicked the tarmac for Shane. Nick pulled enough strings to reel Shane into the San Francisco Field Office. Now together, they were working a case Shane believed was linked to his parents' death.

Shane headed across the street, dodging cars. "I'm going to make contact."

Nick chuckled, "Enjoy. The redhead's one hot little number. Her friend's a real looker too. You sure you don't want to trade places?"

Hell no! "I would, but I have to do this myself. Just take care of Katie." Shane said as he walked into Harrah's.

The sound of slots ringing and voices straining to be heard filled the room. Shane moved across the Casino floor, his gaze flicking through the crowd.

He waited in line at the club behind a Bachelorette party. The women laughed and giggled and flirted with all the men, including Shane. He went along with them, but felt old and very relieved when he finally arrived at the window to pay his cover. He then waited as a twenty something year old with purple hair, a nose ring and tattoo covered arms put a plastic bracelet on his wrist.

The pounding bass of dance music assaulted him as he searched the crowd for Riley. Lucky for him, she was easy to spot. Her lacey white blouse glowed in the strobe lights above the dance floor. Shane's cock pulsed as he watched her ample breasts bounce and her shapely ass sway in time with the beat.

The short skirt and kiss-me-fuck-boots beckoned him. His ever-hardening dick led the way as he shed his leather jacket, dropping it on the rail surrounding the dance floor.

In three long strides he stood before her.

Her eyes widening in surprise at his arrival.

"Care to dance?" he asked, pulling her against his hard chest.

She gasped as her body molded into his and his erection hit her stomach. He felt her shudder and smiled.

Shane had learned to dance as a teenager. His mother believed that every man should know how, so she taught him to waltz and to swing.

Turning her into the light he looked into her eyes. They were a deeper shade of green than his own, more vibrant, captivating.

"I'm Shane," he leaned in to speak in her ear. She shivered when his breath whispered across the tender flesh of her neck.

"Riley," she managed on a strangled breath.

The deer-in-the-headlights look was gone, replaced by a look of smoldering need that matched his. It had been a long time since he experienced chemistry like the sparks sizzling between them. The last woman he'd been involved with was a whore in Florida who helped him gain access to one of the drug lords. Just his luck the woman who might lead him to his parents' killer was Red Hot!

But this wasn't the time for letting his libido call the shots. He could flirt and enjoy the attraction she clearly shared, but he would stay on task. He had to find out what Riley knew about her brother Trevor's activities. If she knew anything at all.

When the song changed to a faster tempo, Shane pulled Riley from the floor, grabbing his jacket as he passed it. He spotted an empty table in the corner and started for it, but Riley protested.

"I'm here with a friend," she shouted and nodded over her shoulder. The blonde from the lounge trailed after them, wearing an amused expression. "Our table's over there," Riley said as she freed herself from his grip and hurried to her table.

Riley took a long swallow of her ice water and tried to get a grip. Her heart pounded in her chest and her stomach continued doing summersaults. She couldn't breathe. "Excuse me, I need to..." she hurried off toward the bathroom.

Grateful for the sitting area just inside the ladies' room, Riley dropped into a chair to catch her breath. She had never reacted so intensely to a man. When she collided with the rock-hard wall of his chest, a slow burning need had begun in her womb.

"Are you okay?" Beth stood in the open doorway, her grin growing. "He has got to be the most beautiful man I have ever seen in my life. His arms are thicker than my thigh. And his butt. Oh my God, Riley did you see that ass?"

Riley giggled. "He is gorgeous, isn't he?" She stood and went to the sink, ran water over a paper towel and wiped her face and neck. She applied lip gloss and immediately her thoughts turned to his full lips and what it would feel like to kiss them. But then she remembered the young blonde he had held close to him earlier and her spirits sank like the Titanic.

"What's wrong," Beth asked.

Riley looked into the mirror at her friends reflection. "Blondie."

"Oh. Her." Beth's eyes turned dark, then brightened. "But he followed you. Maybe she wasn't his girlfriend."

"And maybe she was."

"Well then, I dare you to go ask him." Beth didn't wait for a response. She turned and left the room.

Riley steeled herself and followed her friend back into the club. She'd only had sex with two men in her whole life. She had no experience in dealing with the intense attraction to Shane. He exuded more raw sexuality than any man she'd ever seen.

Shane made eye contact with Riley as soon as she came around the corner. Her stomach did another flip and she forced herself to mask her nervousness behind a smile.

Shane had obviously ordered a bottle of Rombauer and three glasses. He stood and pulled out a chair for Beth, then did the same for Riley, leaving her no choice but to sit beside him.

"Wine ladies?" Shane poured them each a glass, then filled his as he watched the ladies look at one another in surprise. "I noticed that you were drinking Rombauer at the Luxury Lounge."

"You like wine?" Beth asked in shock as she took a long look at his body.

"Yes, I do, but I prefer Cabernet. Silver Oak is one of my favorites."

Riley gasped as heat rushed to her face at the mention of Silver Oak.

"You okay, Red?" He smiled and then turned his attention to Beth. He extended his hand, "Shane Blackstone."

"Beth Fisher." She smiled.

Definitely Nick's type. Cute, hot, and his best intuitive guess? Flirty and dirty.

Shane liked open-minded women, especially in bed, but Beth didn't make his blood pulse like Red did. Something about her brought his caveman instincts to the surface. He wanted to protect her. He wanted to do a lot to her.

But she was his case. He had to be careful.

He turned his high-beam smile on her, staring into mint green eyes. A slow song started and Shane pulled Riley back onto the dance floor. They moved together easily and made small talk as they danced. Shane told Riley he was in town taking care of his sister.

"The blonde in the bar earlier?" Riley asked.

Shane nodded. "She's had a rough time lately. Been drinking too much and getting into trouble."

Relieved by the news, Riley pressed tighter against Shane as the song wound down to an end. Disappointment curled through her when he let go of her. She followed him back to the table and sipped her wine. Beth smiled and asked Shane if he had any hunky friends.

"As a matter of fact, I do," Shane winked at Riley. "Maybe we can all get together for dinner sometime."

Riley nodded at him, then her eyes widened with surprise. A tingle rode up Shane's spine at Riley's expression. He turned as Trevor Snow bore down on them.

This was the last thing he needed. He and Trevor had already had several run-ins. He was a member of the Gym that Shane now owned, and he knew Trevor worked for Joe "Domino" Dominico, the prime suspect in the murder of Susan and Walter Blackstone, Shane's parents.

"Mind if I join you, Riley?" Trevor pulled up a chair and stared across the table at Shane.

He felt the tension rise in Riley. "Do whatever you want Trevor," she shook her head. "You usually do."

Trevor picked up Riley's glass, took a drink and scowled. He waved at a waitress, and ordered a double shot of tequila. Riley hated it when her brother drank tequila. It made him meaner than he already was.

Beth tried to keep things light, but the air grew heavier by the minute. It became apparent that Trevor had no intention of leaving.

Riley leaned over and thanked Shane for the dance and the wine. "I had fun, but I need to get up early."

Shane smiled, kissed her on the cheek and pulled his jacket on. "I'll walk you out."

"That's not necessary." Riley said as she too slid into her coat.

"Of course, it isn't. I want to."

Shane saw Beth and Riley to their car. Like a gentleman, he waited until she belted in before closing the door. He waved as Beth pulled out and drove away.

Snow fell heavily now, and Riley was grateful for Beth's monster four-wheel drive Suburban. She leaned back into the heated leather seat.

"He didn't ask for my number."

"No, but he'll find it." Beth flipped the wipers up to full speed. "He had a hard-on for you. Literally."

Riley laughed. "And how would you know?"

"I had the pleasure of seeing the bulge in his pants. I'm guessing he is *very* well endowed. I must say I am jealous, girlfriend."

Riley's cell phone rang. She pulled it from her clutch, sighing, "What do you want now, Trevor?"

"What's up with the hulk you were with?" The disdain in his voice reminded Riley of why she steered clear of her brother.

"Why Trevor? Since when do you really care what I do and who I do it with?"

"Since now. Stay away from him Riley. He's trouble."

"And you know this, why?"

"Trust me. Stay clear."

"Right, Trevor. Whatever. Goodnight."

"What's Trevor's problem?" Beth asked as she pulled into Riley's drive.

Riley replayed the conversation. "He's an ass. In fact, I think they all are. Why do we even bother?"

"Because we like sex?" Beth asked softly.

Riley laughed. "Yeah. I guess that's it. Thanks for the ride."

Chapter Three

Riley woke with the unpleasant memory of her brother's interference still rolling around in her thoughts. She and Trevor were never close. Her decision to move to Tahoe had nothing to do with the fact that he lived here, but even though they didn't get along, she knew if she needed his help, he would be there for her.

After five miles on the treadmill, she threw a shirt and sweats over her work-out clothes and headed upstairs to her office.

"Alexa, play John Mayer radio," she said as she booted up her laptop. After checking her email, she got to work sketching out scene ideas and tightening up her character worksheets.

Since childhood, Riley wanted to write books. She attempted her first mystery at sixteen, then tried again at twenty-three, but Robert thought her creativity a waste of time. She'd taken a job at a busy San Francisco newspaper writing fluff pieces for the living section. She'd hated it. Her tyrant of a boss sent her to dog shows and cooking classes and charity events. Riley knew she should have been grateful for the opportunity, but the hours sucked, the topics very boring -- to her -- and the society bitches she'd gone to Covington with were often in attendance. That irked the most. Dealing with them after the horrid time in school proved too much for her lower than low self-esteem.

Now, thanks to Robert, Riley had enough money in the bank to take a sabbatical from her journalism career to focus on writing fiction.

This time, Riley planned to write a romance. Her own interests in reading had changed over the years and romance offered such a wide variety of avenues. Besides, romance would be much more fun. Especially the spicy kind. And last night, she hit inspiration head-on.

Gazing out the window at the white landscape, Riley replayed her encounter with Shane. She smiled as she remembered the way his body felt against hers. The way his erection had pressed into her, making her want to have wild sex on the dance floor. Of course, she could think like that now when he was nowhere in sight. At the time, she could only wonder what she would do with so much man.

Riley pulled up the character worksheet for the hunky man in her romantic comedy and made some changes, modeling him after Shane. The outline for her story was almost complete and she looked forward to starting the actual writing. She spent another hour writing a steamy sex scene she may or may not find a use for in her book. By the time she finished, her panties were wet and she was hornier than she'd ever been in her life.

Riley went to the kitchen, poured another cup of coffee wondering if Shane's thoughts today included her.

Her cell phone rang. She reached into the purse she'd had with her last night and pulled the phone out. When she saw Trevor's name on the screen, she hit ignore to silence the ringing and picked up her coffee.

She went back up the stairs, dropped her cell on the desk and took a long sip of coffee.

After an hour or more tweaking her story outline, Riley began writing. She submersed herself in her getting words down and lost all track of time as she moved through three chapters introducing her main characters.

It took Riley a minute to realize the ringing phone. She fumbled to find her cell, but it wasn't the source of the intrusive noise and finally she grabbed up the receiver for the land line. In her confusion and haste, she punched the talk button without checking the caller ID. "Hello?" If it was Trevor again...

"Hey Riley." Her stomach bungee jumped at the sound of Shane's voice. "You kind of rushed off after your brother crashed our party. He seems a bit...uptight."

Riley smiled. "Yeah. Sorry about that. I was having...fun."

"Me too. That's why I called. Have dinner with me tonight."

His deep voice held an edge of something Riley couldn't identify. She didn't know him at all, but there was something under the surface. "I don't know, Shane. I appreciate the offer." Riley wanted to say yes, but the man terrified her on many levels. She found him intriguing, handsome as the devil in disguise, but...

"If you don't have dinner with me, I think I'll go crazy. Besides," his voice lowered to almost a whisper that set her insides afire. "I have something you want." The innuendo made her tighten in her innermost center. *I'll just bet you do.*

Riley couldn't stop the moans' escape.

He chuckled. "Your wallet."

"Oh my, God. No. How?" No wonder he hadn't asked for her number. He knew where she lived. Her number would be easy to find, especially since it was listed in the phone book.

"When you got in the car it fell from your purse." His voice deepened. "I could have run after you, but I thought I might need leverage. I guess I was right."

"Not necessarily." She grinned. Two could play. And she had a feeling it might be lots of fun. "There's nothing in there but my license and a twenty. I could refuse, and go to the DMV and get a new one."

"And break my heart at the same time?" A playful edge laced his voice, making her think of his lips and big hands. "Come on, Riley. Do I have to beg?"

Her smile widened. "Or I could call the police and tell them you stole my wallet."

"You're killing me. Just say yes. Your choice. Anywhere you want to go."

Now that was an offer too hard to refuse. "Well, I've always wanted to try *The Sage Room*."

"Perfect. I've already made the reservation. See you at seven-thirty."

And he was gone.

The dial tone bleeped as she stared at the phone. How had he known she'd want to go to *The Sage Room*?

She zeroed in on the digital clock in the display window of her phone. Still in shock.

Six o'clock.

Shit.

Riley dropped the phone, saved her document and shut down her laptop. She dashed down the stairs and into her bedroom, ripped off her Forty-niner jersey, shed her sports bra, and slinked out of the sweats she pulled on over her running shorts, leaving puddles of clothing in the trail to her bathroom.

She cranked on the shower, climbing in gasping as cold water slowly turned warm, then hot.

How would she handle an evening with Shane the Hunk McHottie? She giggled. He was HOT -- branding iron hot -- with eyes that pulled you under, into...ecstasy, she'd bet. Then, she reminded herself that she wasn't a loose, brazen slut.

She slowly lathered her breasts and her nipples quickly grew taut with wanting. She felt her insides turn liquid as she fantasized about Shane's soap slicked hands smoothing over her skin. Her hand went to her center, finding the sensitive flesh at her core. She quickly moved on, wanting to save her excitement for him, because maybe tonight she would be that wanton slut who took risks and actually had fun. Maybe she would try out the scenes she planned to write for her book. After all, research was so important when writing a book.

Once rinsed, she wrapped her hair in a towel, applied a lavender scrub and rinsed again.

What to wear became her obsession. She didn't want to look easy, but she wanted to look... delicious. Though she had never felt delicious. Robert had grunted and panted and moaned during sex, but never made her feel delicious. The idea of Shane wanting her naked in bed filled her mind and turned her bones to gel.

Ever since she and Beth had teased about getting him in bed, it was all she could think about, and now she was preparing for a date.

With him.

She applied moisturizer to her face, slicked on antiperspirant and dragged curling gel through her unruly curls. She would apply her make-up after she dressed.

She tore through her closet, looking for just the right outfit, and after four wardrobe changes, she settled on a simple green silk sheathe. It was tight, and she wondered if it outlined too-thick curves, but the color highlighted her hair and eyes. She would just have to watch how much she ate.

Sliding into matching Jimmy Choo heels -- shoes were her one true obsession -- she returned to the bathroom to apply a light coat of make-up.

Riley heard the garage door go up, then someone stomping up the stairs. Beth was the only person with a key, actually a garage door opener because of the house's style, and in the winter weather, it was easier to pull into the garage and come up through the house. And then there was the fact that Beth was at Riley's house more than her own home.

Riley stepped out of the bathroom as Beth came into the bedroom.

"Wow. You look gorgeous!" Beth dropped down on the bed. "Shane?"

Riley grinned. "Yeah." She spun around in a Cinderella circle. "Is the dress too tight?" She knew Beth would never lie to her.

"Hell no. It looks fabulous on you." Beth looked her friend over critically. "You'll definitely get lucky tonight. Are you planning to bring him back here?"

"No!" Riley felt the heat rise in her face. "I hardly know him. It's way too soon to consider that."

"Uh, huh." Beth shook her head, "then you'd better find something else to wear. No hot-blooded male, specially one who already seems to want you, would take no for an answer with you in that dress."

"You think he'll like it?" Riley turned to the full-length mirror, checking her reflection with apprehension.

"Trust me, Riley. He'll love it." Her friend jumped from the edge of the bed and stood behind Riley. He won't even make it through the appetizer."

Filled with a strong dose of Female Power, Riley did another quick pirouette.

"How did he get your number anyway?" Beth asked as Riley fought the doubt from years of low self-esteem.

"Turns out I dropped my little wallet with my ID and cab fare."

"Ah." Beth had the same mini wallet in her purse. "I knew he'd find you. He looked at you like his next meal last night."

Riley looked down at her figure in the green dress. Nerves made her not even close to knobby knees knock. "Well, in that case maybe I should tone it down a bit."

"Don't you dare," Beth said as she dragged Riley to the coat closet, "Go. Have fun." She thrust a long black coat at her friend, "I'm going to hang out here for a while and watch your big TV and drink your wine, but I'll be gone before you get back."

"What's wrong with your house?" Riley asked, even though she knew the answer.

"You're TV is bigger than mine. Now, go. Have fun."

Chapter Four

Shane spent the day with Katie. They went to breakfast, then drove over the hill, into the Carson Valley to do some shopping.

On the way home, they laughed a lot. It almost felt as though things were normal until Katie asked about Riley.

"Is she your girlfriend?"

Girlfriend? Shane hadn't had a girlfriend since high-school, except for the girl he'd met in South Carolina, whom he once thought he would marry. Something about serving in the military made a guy long for marriage. The relationship didn't last. She sucked at being alone and slept around. Shane found out and dumped her. Once he started college, he had his share of sex, but no serious relationships. He didn't believe in happily-ever-after. What man did? Shane certainly didn't know any happily-ever-after marriages. Except for his parents. They were the epitome of the Cleavers. Perfect home, perfect marriage, perfect children. Not that Shane considered himself perfect, but his parents had done a helluva job raising he and Katie.

Most of Shane's friends growing up came from broken homes and very few of his military buddies had families intact. Happily-ever-after was for fairy tales.

Riley certainly caught his interest in more ways than one. But the one that counted most drove him. Revenge.

Shane thought he should lie, but decided at the end of the day, the truth would out. "No. I do like her and plan to spend time with her, but the truth is she is the sister of someone I think may know who killed Mom and Dad."

Katie sucked in a breath, her face going white as a bleached sheet. Shane feared her catatonic state would follow. "Then you need to do whatever it takes," she finally said in a quiet voice.

She put in her ear buds locked in her own little world the rest of the way home.

Nick came outside when they got back and helped unload the car.

"She seems okay today," Nick mentioned while Katie went into the kitchen to make lunch for them.

"She pops in and out of her moods. We talked about Riley. She asked if she was my girlfriend."

Nick smiled. "Whadya tell her?"

"The truth. She told me to do what I needed to do."

"Out of the mouths of babes."

"Thanks for being here for us." Shane slapped Nick on the shoulder. "Getting the brass to give us time to get this done was a huge win. I appreciate it, Nick."

Nick pushed Shane away. "Don't go getting all mushy on me, bro."

Shane chuckled. Nick's picture should be in the dictionary beside the word friend. Loyal, caring and cutting through the bullshit were some of Nick's best qualities.

Nick made light of it even though getting their superiors to allow them to take the next three months off, use DEA resources and equipment was no small feat. Unheard of actually. But they wanted Domino taken out of commission almost as badly as Shane.

Having a huge inheritance allowed Shane the freedom to take time off. That Nick didn't hesitate to let Shane support him during their 'leave', was kind of comical. Nick had said, "You can't spend that much money in five lifetimes, so I figure what's the harm".

Shane only inherited a quarter of a million, a house and a thriving business. Nick was right on the one hand. It was a great deal of money and Shane wouldn't spend it in his lifetime. He didn't get worked up about things. Could care less about them really. As long as he had a car, a roof and food in the fridge, he'd be happy. Oh yeah, and sex with a hot lady on occasion.

Truth be told, Nick came from money, lots of it. He didn't need anything from Shane.

Shane snapped back to attention. "I'm hungry. Let's see what Katie's making."

"Sounds like a plan."

Nick followed Shane into the kitchen. Katie had sandwich makings spread out across the granite counter top.

"What kind do you want guys? I have the bread slathered with mustard and mayo, you need to finish building your own lunch."

"Yes, ma'am."

Katie smiled and took her meal to the table.

The three laughed and joked throughout lunch and again Shane wondered at her swinging moods.

He ran to the gym, worked out, did some paperwork and called Riley to invite her to dinner. He even managed a quick call to the psychiatrist Katie had been seeing since Shane returned from his assignment in Florida.

After his shower he dressed in black Dockers and a mint green dress shirt. He checked all the doors and windows one more time before grabbing his keys and coat.

Katie was stretched out on the couch, three DVD's and a giant bowl of popcorn to keep her company. He was relieved that her mood was so much better today. The doctor said her memory would come back, and that until it did, she would be easily distracted and prone to serious mood swings. Sometimes Shane wished she would get her memory back -- maybe then he would have the proof he needed to take out the bastard who killed his parents. But the risk to her sanity wasn't worth it. He'd find another way.

Nick was closeted away in the study, doing some research on his ever-present laptop. "I'm out of here," Shane said from the doorway.

"You have the wallet?"

"Yes. I'll make sure another listening device is planted on her cell phone. Once I'm in the house, I'll plant the other three."

"You sure you're up for this?" Nick frowned at Shane. "Your obvious attraction to her may be too much of a distraction. I can take over."

Shane's hands tightened into fists. "I'm fine." It annoyed the hell of him that his friend knew him so well. He *was* too damned attracted to Riley, but he was more determined to meet out his specialized brand of justice. "I can handle this, and her. You do your fucking part and everything will be fine."

Nick laughed. "Yeah. Fine. See you later, bro."

Shane drove too fast through the icy streets as he thought about how hard his dad had tried to take down Domino. He had done everything he could to protect his family. Everything except telling Shane the truth. If he had, maybe Shane could have helped, could've prevented the tragedy his family had suffered. Now, he had to live with the pain of not being there for his sister, the betrayal he felt over his dad's lack of trust in him, and the emptiness he felt every time he walked into his childhood home.

He parked in the covered garage below Harrah's and took the elevator to the top floor. His groin tightened as his gaze fell on Riley. He wished she'd picked a more casual restaurant. He didn't know if he could endure an evening of watching her move in that soft, sexy dress. He planned his attire well. His straight cut dress shirt wasn't intended to be tucked in so most of his reaction to the beautiful woman that would be his date for the evening was covered.

He came up silently beside her. "You look amazing." He turned her so she faced him. "Definitely, amazing."

Riley's senses went on high alert. Her nerve endings tingled. The look in his eyes primal, making her feel wanton. "Thank you. You look pretty nice yourself."

He flashed a mega-watt smile that set her insides on fire. *Damn, he was handsome, and rugged, and sexy, and made her want to rip her clothes off and beg for...everything.*

They were taken to a secluded table; it was elegant and romantic and Riley was so nervous and so excited all at once. She was in hypersensitive mode.

Once seated, Shane ordered a bottle of Silver Oak, his favorite Cabernet.

Liquid Sex--I'm in big trouble.

Riley picked up the menu and pretended to study it. She couldn't possibly eat with the battalion of butterflies battling in her stomach. She really needed to get hold of herself.

Words became clearer and Riley decided that if she was drinking Silver Oak, she would make sure she matched it with the right dish. The dress wasn't that tight after all, and she was already feeling bolder than she ever imagined she would, and she hadn't even had a drink.

He lowered her menu, and there he was, staring at her, his smile causing tingles and wingles -- whatever they were but she knew she was feeling them. The smoldering look lit her insides to molten levels. "What looks good to you?" He asked in a velvety smooth voice that should be outlawed in public.

OhmyGod, you so look good to me I'm embarrassed by the fact that I want to rip your clothes off right here in this restaurant. But Riley kicked the its-been-way-too-long-and-I'm-horny-and-you-are-so-hot thoughts from her brain and remembered that a beef dish would be the right choice for Silver Oak and finally answered, "I'm thinking the medallions."

He smiled again, and the room brightened. "Great choice. If you're willing to share, I'll order the Lamb in Cherry Sauce." He licked his lips.

"Okay." Riley answered as she stared at his mouth. She couldn't help it. She wanted to kiss him. Bad.

"Great. Appetizer?" His stare sent sparks into her center.

Before she could manage a coherent thought, the waiter arrived with their wine. He opened the bottle, handed the cork to Shane. After a silent okay, the waiter poured, waited until Shane tasted then nodded, then he filled both glasses. He announced the specials, including Oysters Rockefeller.

Shane wondered if he had jumped into quicksand without a long branch to grab hold of. Riley sparked with energy, looked too damn sexy for words and now the waiter had offered them oysters. He didn't need an aphrodisiac. Riley was the strongest one he'd experienced. Ever. "That'd be great," he heard himself say as the waiter nodded and quickly disappeared.

This is going to be a long night. Shane straightened, lifted his glass and sipped his wine. "How long have you been in Tahoe," he asked, fighting to stay on task.

Riley squiggled in her seat. Her libido raged like Niagara - Oh God. Viagra - Niagara. She could feel heat sweep through her body. He had asked her a question but all she could think about was how all that seemingly hard muscle would look without the soft fabric that had the pleasure of dancing across his chest. She smiled and forced her brain back to the conversation.

"My parents have owned a home here for years, they split their time between here and San Francisco, I moved up a few months ago." If he continued to stare at her with those mesmerizing eyes, she would have to excuse herself or have an orgasm right where she sat. Deflect. "How about you?"

"All my life, except while I was in the Military, but every chance I had, I came home." He didn't mention the DEA, or his parents and their death. He needed to stay away from that subject, for lots of reasons. "So, what do you do to keep busy?"

I know what I would like to do to keep busy. "I used to write fluff for a big newspaper. Even dabbled in writing an advice column." She was going insane. "But now I am lucky enough to work from home. I'm trying my hand at a novel."

"An advice column, huh? What kind of advice do you give?" He grinned, that Cheshire Cat kind of grin that split his face and Riley thought he had to be the sexiest man she had ever seen.

"Relationship advice."

Shane leaned forward, "what advice do you have for our developing relationship?"

"I think...I want...sex." There. She said it. And based on the return of the Cheshire smile, she actually believed that he wanted it too. "Okay, now you have to say something, because I cannot believe I just said that out loud and I feel like I should maybe slide down under the table and disappear through the floor."

Shane thought she was the most adorable creature he had ever seen. The flush that crept into her face at her admission, the abject fear and embarrassment as she waited for his response was too tempting. But he leaned in closer, until he could feel her breath. He brushed his lips lightly over hers and whispered, "Me too."

The waiter appeared with their oysters and he both thanked and cursed whatever guardian watched over him. He needed to distance himself from the incredibly sexy woman next to him. The brief contact with her was like a lightning strike to his groin. No matter what information he needed from her, he knew in his soul that he would have to fuck her to get this driving lust out of his system so that he could think straight.

He put a couple of oysters on a plate and handed it to Riley, then served himself. "My mouth is watering, but they feel pretty hot." Shane took a sip of wine. "So where were we, I need a diversion from my hunger."

Riley laughed out loud. The idea of diverting her hunger seemed impossible at this point. The taste of Silver Oak on Shane's lips was testament to the nickname 'liquid sex'. She could feel the moisture building between her legs as the seconds ticked by. "I don't think anything can divert my hunger at this point." And when she realized the connotation in her statement, she quickly picked up her fork, loosened the oyster from its shell and slid the delicious, but still hot morsel into her mouth. "Hmmm. This is incredible," she said as she licked her lips. "Go on, try one."

Shane lifted the oyster, shell and all, to his mouth and held it there as he stared at her. His tongue darted out to test the temperature and Riley squirmed, never breaking eye contact. Her vagina buzzed with excitement as he slowly sucked the oyster from the shell.

"You have to stop that." Riley said as his tongue circled his gorgeous lips seductively.

He grinned. "I don't know if I can make it through an entire dinner. I want you now."

And he did. His cock was straining to be freed. He tried to push down the desire that speared through him but something about Riley Snow captivated him, drew him in in a way that was foreign and scary and yet pumped his adrenaline -- and his cock -- into hyper-drive.

He sucked down a couple more oysters, offered Riley the last one and took a long drink of water. Maybe if he dumped the ice water into his lap his throbbing dick would shrink back to a manageable size and he could concentrate on getting the information he needed from Riley. But she drew the shell to her lips and outdid his seductive sucking of oyster into mouth and caused his heartbeat to quicken and his dick to throb harder. He had to get control.

Like magic, the waiter appeared, cleared off the appetizer plates and promised to return in a few moments with their main courses. Thank God. Shane needed release. He could wolf down his food, order desert to go and if necessary, rent a room in the hotel below them -- maybe he would get that handled now. He forced his dick to stand down and excused himself.

Riley watched Shane move across the dining room. He had the physique of a warrior. The tight butt, lean waist, and broad shoulders. She wasn't a size four but she guessed he could bench press her easily. She wanted him to throw her around and do her every which way imaginable. She thought of Beth's prediction that Shane wouldn't make it through the appetizers. Wrong. Riley hadn't even made it to the table before she wanted to throw *him* down.

It was insane. She had never acted so shamelessly in her life and she didn't care. She'd admitted, out loud, that she wanted to have sex. Good God. She wanted Shane badly and she knew deep down in her soul that as soon as the meal was over, she would have him.

The waiter materialized at her side refilling both of their wineglasses just as Shane returned.

The look in his eyes as he sat caused a quick shiver to run down Riley's back. He was just so damned good looking it should be illegal. In fact, why was he single? "Are you married?" the words tumbled unbidden from her mouth.

Shock turned to amusement. "No. Never been married. Came close once but she couldn't handle the military life. Always moving, alone a lot while I was deployed. Not many women can handle it. How about you?"

"Divorced." Not a subject Riley wanted to discuss at the moment.

"Really?"

His response was like a hot poker to her ass, and she found herself explaining the naked bouncing butt in her bed. He laughed a deep belly laugh that had heads turning from every nearby table.

Riley smiled. "I guess it is a cliché isn't it. Wife comes home to find her husband doing the horizontal mambo with a barely graduated from jail bait babe. It could be a Lifetime movie." Shane didn't seem the type to watch Lifetime, let alone know about the kind of movies the network aired.

He intrigued her.

Dinner arrived saving her from needing to explain further.

Shane watched as she took a bite of her tenderloin. Her moan of pleasure caused Mr. Happy to awaken. Shane enjoyed watching her eat. She was dainty and yet managed to shovel her food into her mouth with a speed that defied logic. She passed a forkful to him. The tender meat melted in his mouth.

He reciprocated and she made a dick raising sound as she savored the bite of lamb. He didn't even try to converse, but instead ate until his plate was empty.

He watched Riley take the last bite of garlic mashed potato. "How about desert to go?" He asked before she could set her fork down.

"Sounds good. Where are we going?" Riley leaned back in her chair and sipped her wine.

"Downstairs." Shane reached into the pocket of his shirt and withdrew a card key. "Room 1441 to be exact."

Her eyebrows rose but she smiled. "Can we have desert delivered?"

"Gorgeous and brilliant. Boy, am I lucky or what?"

Shane waived the waiter over, ordered a chocolate volcano cake, another bottle of Silver Oak and chocolate dipped strawberries.

"Shall we?" He asked, extending his hand as he stood.

When her hand touched his, a jolt of heat rushed through his bloodstream straight to his dick. He nearly dragged her to the elevator. The door closed, opening seconds later. Shane led her down the short hallway, turned the corner and ran his card key through the slot. They stepped into a hotel suite and Riley stopped in her tracks.

"Oh my God. This is beautiful. Shane it must be so expensive." She couldn't imagine an ex-military guy being able to afford this room and the dinner, especially with two bottles of Silver Oak on the tab.

"Trust me, it's not a big deal." He turned her around and pulled her close. "I have a feeling you're well worth it."

Riley felt the hardness of his erection as soon as he pulled her to him and her brain turned to mush. His eyes darkened as he leaned down and slanted his mouth over hers. The contact electric. She opened her mouth in invitation and when their tongues touched Riley felt her vagina contract and wondered if she could keep from coming right then and there.

He sparred with her tongue and pulled away, breathless. "I don't know about you but I need you naked. Now."

He reached behind her back and unzipped her dress. It slid to the floor, leaving her in matching green silk bra and panties. "Beautiful." His primal stare heated her from the inside out.

She ignored the shirt and went straight for the button on his pants. But his hands were pushing hers away and in a fluid motion his pants were gone and his beautiful, long, thick erection was pushing against her belly.

He put his hands on her waist and slid them downward, catching her panties on the downward stroke and dragging them down her legs until they hit the floor. She started to step out of them but was lifted upward and slowly lowered onto his waiting cock.

"Oh. My. God." She whispered as he slowly entered her while backing her toward the nearest wall. He pushed until he was completely inside her, until his length touched her cervix. She struggled to keep from shouting out. He felt so good inside her, stretching her to unknown limits with his thickness. She really thought she would shatter. He magically unhooked her bra and lowered his mouth over a straining nipple.

She inhaled sharply. "I...Shane?"

He started to pull out but she grabbed his tight ass and pulled him back.

He laughed. "You want more?"

"Yes, please." She pushed toward him and he met her with a quick thrust of his own. Then he pulled out.

She felt empty without him.

"I can't believe I almost forgot this."

Riley watched as he dug a condom out of his shirt pocket. He tore the silver packet open and stretched the latex over his incredible length.

She reached for it and guided him back to her opening. "Now." She demanded.

He thrust inside her in one quick stroke, catching her moan with his mouth. He kissed her, darting his tongue inside in and out in unison with the thrust of his dick. Riley shuttered and when she contracted around his cock, he groaned and came with her. She felt him pulsing over and over again.

Her shudders rocked her in waves and she thought she might cry with the wonder of it. She squeezed her eyes tightly shut to stop the threatening tears. It...he was amazing. Riley had never had such an intense orgasm in her life. And so easily.

When she could breathe again, she opened her eyes. Shane was looking at her with his own brand of wonder. "Wow," she said and smiled at him. "That was...wow."

He chuckled. "You're dripping all over me," he said as he moved inside her.

"And you're still hard. Can I have another ride?"

"Of course. But I think maybe we should find a more comfortable position."

She wrapped her legs tightly around him as he carried her to the next room where a huge bed awaited. She pulled the covers down as he lowered her and as soon as her back hit the bed, he began a slow dance inside her. They moved together easily, and within minutes Riley felt the tightening that signaled another mind-blowing orgasm. When she came, she screamed and this time Shane wasn't able to quiet her with a kiss because he was once again in synch with her. He tensed and she watched his face as he shuttered.

She reached up and gently touched his cheek. "You're superb."

He smiled and collapsed on her, shifting just enough so that she didn't have his full weight on her.

"So are you."

Shane pushed himself up. He looked down at her and felt a tenderness he had never before felt. It scared him and yet he wanted more of her. He leaned close and kissed her gently. "I'll be right back." He pulled out and went to the bathroom.

He removed the condom, tossing it in the trash and rinsed himself. After grabbing a robe from behind the door, Shane ran warm water over a washcloth and took it to Riley.

"Dessert will be here in a few minutes." He put on the robe. "Do you want a glass of water?"

"That would be great. Thanks."

As if on cue, room service arrived. Shane left Riley to clean up. He picked up their discarded clothes on the way to the door, tipped the waiter and locked up behind him. He heard the shower going and decided he should take advantage of the chance to check in with Nick.

He hit the contact Icon for Nick and paced the room.

"How's it going?" Nick asked.

"Not as expected. I won't be home tonight."

Nick chuckled, "Red is pretty hot I take it."

"You have no idea." Shane didn't want to consider just how hot or how good things were. This was supposed to be a case, albeit the most important one of his life, and it was turning out to be mind-blowing in more ways than one. "Everything quiet there?"

"Yeah. We're good. Talk to you tomorrow. And Shane?"

"Yeah?"

"Have fun."

Before he could respond, Nick was gone.

Shane grinned. *Shouldn't be a problem with that.*

Chapter Five

R iley rinsed off, then decided to enjoy the huge Jacuzzi. She dumped vanilla scented body wash in the tub, turned the water on full and climbed in.

Sinking into the bubbles, Riley submersed all but her head, which she leaned against the conveniently padded tub edge. She thought perhaps she had died and gone to heaven.

Shane came through the door pushing the dessert cart. He had discarded his robe along the way and when he was free of the cart she watched as Shane's beautiful cock grew hard again.

"Oh, boy. You are a stud, aren't you?" She reached for his erection, loving the silky feel of his skin. She pulled him closer and licked around the corona. Smiling at the sharp intake of breath. Feeling that Female Power surge through her, she took him in her mouth. He sighed and held her head between his hands as she sucked and licked and teased his magnificent dick.

She could feel him grow in her mouth and wondered how the already huge member could possibly get larger and decided that it must be her causing the reaction. That made her want more and she took him so far into her mouth she feared she would choke. She had never really been big on giving blow jobs -- which she now thought a ridiculous name because it involved very little blowing-- but with Shane it was addicting.

Even when she heard his breathing become more rapid and felt his cock throb in her mouth she continued to suck until he finally forced her to release him. He climbed in the tub, lifted her to its edge and pushed himself into her.

"Oh, yes!" He said as he pumped into her pulsing vagina, pulling out just as he began to come.

She watched in fascination as he pulled at his cock, squeezing every drop of semen from it and moaning with pleasure. It was such a turn on that she felt herself dripping with excitement.

"Your turn," he said as he settled her on the edge of the tub and knelt in front of her. He licked his way down her body. When he found her clit, she shivered and pushed her hips in an effort to strengthen the contact. He inserted a finger into her dripping pussy and pulled at her clit with his lips.

"Oh, God. Shane...I...am...so...going...to" and she exploded in another earth-shattering climax as he continued to suck and lick. When the quaking turned to tremors, he entered her and thought that he would die from the pleasure; tight, hot and still constricting. Shane couldn't remember when he had been so totally driven by lust. He wondered if she had slipped him a Viagra.

No man could possibly get it up so quickly and so often. But he had. He pounded into her, and she somehow found the energy to meet his thrusts with an upward motion of her pelvis. She was insatiable. He was rock hard. With every forward push, she moaned, leaning her head back while pushing her pelvis upward.

"My God, Red. You're so hot."

He grabbed her butt, a cheek in each hand, helping him drive deeper. The groan that sneaked past her lips was his undoing. He exploded into her. He tensed with his release as he realized he'd forgotten the condom, but the thought was fleeting because he continued to spasm in orgasm as she began to clench her vaginal walls around his throbbing cock, sucking every last bit of semen from him.

And then she shattered. The feel of her wrapping around him as her body released was euphoric. His dick hardened as the intensity of her orgasm surrounded him. She pushed toward him, her body tightening, flexing, and tightening again. Her breath stopped, then a jolt shook her and she gasped.

He watched the torturous pleasure on her face, and then a tear trickled down her cheek. He held her tightly until her breathing settled into a normal pace, terrified at the intensity of the experience -- of her tears.

"That was the most amazing, intense orgasm I have ever had." Her words were just a whisper. She kissed his neck, his cheek, his mouth. "Thank you."

He looked into her eyes and shuddered. *Oh man I am in trouble.* "My pleasure." He smiled and slowly lowered them into the tub until they were submerged in bubbles and roiling water.

Minutes passed as Riley rested her head on his chest. He didn't want to move, but feared they would drown if they didn't make their way to the bed. "Red? You awake?"

"Hmmm." She murmured, tickling his chest with her breath and damn if he didn't feel himself growing hard inside her. The ease at which he grew hard, especially so quickly shocked him. Again, he wondered at the possibility that a man could come so many times in such a short period.

He felt her smile, then her hips began to move. She looked up at him and something in her eyes made his heart skip. Their lips met in a slow, lazy kiss as they continued to move together. She broke away first, lifting her hands to his shoulders and standing in the tub to allow for a more aggressive position. He obliged, grabbing her hips and steadying her as she rode him. The pace quickened until they hit a breakneck speed into which they vaulted together over the top of another tremendous orgasm.

As she lay sated and somewhat sore in bed beside Shane, Riley wondered if anyone had ever died from too much pleasure. Her body still quivered from her last orgasm -- the fourteenth, or maybe eighteenth, she really had lost track -- she curled into Shane's side, one leg draped over his lower half, her head on his chest.

She didn't know about Prince Charming, but she had certainly found a magnificent stallion. She never wanted the night to end. She didn't know that sex could be so spectacular. Didn't know she was capable of such intense-- and let's face it -- so many damned orgasms. Of course, she was spoiled now, forever. She couldn't imagine any-one ever being this good. Not that her bed post had many notches on it but she read a lot, and shared everything with Beth, and Beth had never talked about sex like this.

Caressing the hard contours of his stomach in slow circles, Riley smiled as a sigh slipped past his lips. For all the hard muscle and bone, his skin was soft and hot. Riley could go on touching him like this -- and in other ways -- all night. But very little was left of the night, she noticed when she looked at the digital clock on the bedside table. 4:23 A.M.

She really needed to get some sleep. Her parents were coming up this weekend, and Riley had a thousand things to do. She also needed to write three columns. Ideas swirled through her mind until sleep took over and then she dreamed of Shane.

The smell of coffee and bacon finally broke through Riley's con-sciousness. She forced her eyes open and was rewarded with the sight of Shane standing beside the bed wearing nothing but a hard on and a smile.

"Non-Fat Vanilla Latte with three shots and no whip." He said, extending her most favorite drink -- aside from her new favorite which was now Silver Oak Cabernet.

"How did you know?" She sipped the coffee as he turned to pull the room service cart closer to the bed. "This is exactly what I always order. I'm addicted to these things."

He grinned, snatched a piece of bacon and crunched on it. *He had to be the sexiest man she had ever met.* "Well, I think you deserve a reward. I'll be right back."

Without any modesty, which really surprised Riley, she went into the bathroom, smiled at the brand-new toothbrush on the counter and quickly, like in under two minutes, showered, brushed her teeth, made a minor attempt to tame her crazy hair.

When she made it back to the bed, Shane handed her a plate of scrambled eggs, bacon and fruit. "I'm starving. Thank you." She kissed him and dug in. The second she finished eating, which was about thirty seconds after his plate was set aside, she reached for him.

"And now for your reward." Riley kissed Shane hard on the lips and wasted no time going after what she wanted -- his beautiful dick in her mouth. "And my dessert." She said as she took his length into her mouth. "Hmmm." She looked into his eyes as she licked her tongue along the shaft. "You know what this needs?"

The heat in his eyes intensified. He reached behind his pillow and pulled out a can of whipped cream. "This?" He said, with a look of raw desire.

"Are you psychic or something?" She took the can, shook it and then pulled the cap off. "If you are, then you know what's about to happen."

She sprayed a dollop of whipped cream on the tip of his cock and ever so lightly, licked it off, then pulled him into her mouth to clean the residue off.

"Red, you're gonna kill me."

"Uh huh."

She sprayed a line along the vein on the underside of him and licked it off. She sprayed and played and sucked and licked until Shane thought he would truly die of pleasure. When he couldn't stand anymore, he grabbed the can and in one smooth motion, rolled her over and sprayed each nipple.

The entire can of whipped cream devoured, three earth-shattering orgasms and an hour later, they made their way to the bathroom and showered. Check out time had passed, and Shane needed to get moving. He could easily hide away in this haven of pleasure for days. Aside from having the best sex ever, he hadn't learned anything. He needed some distance from Riley so he could think clearly.

Shane dressed and left Riley to finish getting ready. He checked his cell phone for missed calls, saw two from Nick and hit send.

"Nice of you to check in, stud. How was your night?"

"I don't kiss and tell. What's up?"

"Trevor's cell phone has calls to Dominico's club dating back to two-thousand-five. Appears he is a longtime employee."

"Interesting, but not enough. What about his email?"

"Nothing so far, but without getting onto his computer I can't determine if he has any other email addresses. Did you get to plant any devices?"

Riley came into room and Shane's heart skipped. "I'll get back to you on that." He ended the call, dropped the phone on the couch and went to Riley.

"I had an amazing night." He kissed her, long and well. "Can I call you later?"

"Please do." She thrust her hips toward him.

"Count on it." He placed his hands on her butt and pulled her against him. "I'll save this for you." He was hard and wanting her again, but he needed to get home.

He kissed her one last time and pulled away. "We really need to go before I lose my self-control."

She giggled, gathered up her purse, slipped into her coat and followed Shane out the door. When they got to the parking garage, he helped her into her car, kissed her again and waved as she drove off.

Chapter Six

Riley turned right and began climbing Kingsbury Grade. She lived at the seven-thousand-foot mark. Snow had fallen throughout the night and the roads were still sloppy. She checked the traction control just as her Bluetooth connected. The console display showed Beth Fisher and Riley hit the talk button on her steering wheel.

"Hey."

"Hey yourself. I would've called sooner but I got tied up early this morning and didn't want to wake you." Beth knew Riley loved her sleep. "How was dinner?"

"Nice." Riley smiled, knowing how much Beth would hate her reluctance to share. But she couldn't resist. Normally, Beth had the stories to tell.

"Oh boy. You slept with him, didn't you?"

Okay, so Beth knew her well and wasn't falling for it. "Yeah. About a hundred times."

"No way."

Riley quivered just thinking about it. "Yes way. I had at least twenty orgasms in the last sixteen hours. And by the way, I have never had orgasms as intense or long lasting."

"No way." Beth wasn't the least bit afraid to share her experience.

"Yes, way. He was amazing. Every time I think about him, I get all wet."

"Okay, I can't stand it. Need details. I'm coming over. What do you want for lunch?"

"Nothing. I just had a big breakfast and I really want to make some notes and get to work on my book. I have some really great ideas rolling around in my head. Then I have to clean up the house so I can take the weekend off and hang with the folks." Riley pulled into her driveway, punched the remote for the garage door opener and watched the door roll up. "How about dinner? I should be too tired to write a complete sentence by then."

"Deal. I'll bring the food."

Riley pulled into the garage. "See you then."

The house was a four-story Chalet. Riley climbed a few steps, hit the wall switch that sent the garage door down and then opened a door onto the second-floor mud and laundry room. She made her way up the long staircase to the main living area, which consisted of a large sunny kitchen, dining room, living room, small bath and a very large master bedroom complete with a large Jacuzzi tub and shower. The bedroom was her pride and joy: her sanctuary.

Riley hung her jacket in the walk-in closet and stripped out of her dress, choosing a pair of cozy sweats and her favorite slippers. Once comfy, she grabbed a bottle of water from the fridge and headed to the fourth floor: A guest bedroom, another bathroom and her office. Plants hung from the A-framed ceiling, while several tall fichus trees sat strategically on the floor. Bookcases held thousands of paperbacks and hardcovers, both fiction and non-fiction.

A large cherry wood table doubled as her desk. Riley booted up her laptop as she dropped into a very comfortable high-backed leather chair. As the screen went through startup gyrations, she stared out the window.

Having not been sexually active in her younger days Riley wondered if she'd been too easy last night. She'd never slept with a guy on the first date.

Even though she worked out daily, she wasn't a hard body, slim, supermodel size four. More like a soft, curvy could probably stand to lose another ten pounds, kind of size ten. But Shane really seemed to love her body. After all, he had worshipped it all night long. Umpteen orgasms -- highly intense orgasms -- she quivered as she remembered the first time Shane had licked her. Damn but he knew how to make a girl squirm.

Riley forced her mind away from Shane -- well kind of -- and opened a new word document. She figured she should write a few steamy sex scenes while the memories of last night rolled around in her head. She understood the word obsession now. She wanted to feel Shane's hands and lips and tongue on her body. Now.

Somewhere in her story, her main character would feel this way about the hot hero. Riley began with a hot sex scene, then rambled on about obsession and sense of self and not losing yourself in a man.

After three pages, she reviewed her work. It was nonsense. Three pages of rambling on about independence and taking care of self and a bunch of other, psycho-babble-mumbo-jumbo. But she had a feeling that somewhere in the nonsense she would find something to work with.

The phone rang and Riley nearly knocked the chair over in an effort to get to it.

"Hello?" She fell back into the chair.

"Hi."

Her stomach did a little back flip.

"Hi, yourself."

"What are you doing?" Riley squirmed at the innuendo in his tone.

"Trying to write, but I can't concentrate." *OhmyGod. I said that out loud.*

He chuckled. "Neither can I. How about dinner?"

"Can't. Having dinner with Beth." She really wished she hadn't made those plans now. But then, isn't that exactly what she was trying to write about? Not losing yourself in *him*.

"Okay, then dessert. Strawberries, chocolate, whipped cream?" His tone caused her vagina to contract as heat raced upward.

"I don't know, Shane. I really do have to get some work done."

"No problem. You work. I promise to be good."

She could imagine the laughter dancing in his eyes. "Let's see how much work I get done today. Can I call you later?"

"Nine o'clock, then?"

Riley laughed. "You're incorrigible, I'll call you later."

"A guy has to try."

"Talk to you later?"

"Can't wait."

Riley ended the call but saved his number in her phone.

After reviewing her earlier rambling, she managed to write two Chapters. "*Don't Get Sucked In*" and "*Leashes are For Dogs*". The focus of letting your life become overrun by a man, clearly and concisely addressed with just the right amount of sarcasm dominated both. Now if she could take her own advice. But in her book, the boy would get the girl. And truth be told? She wanted this guy!

After shutting down the computer, she searched her closet for the right, hang-out-around-the-house-but-still-look-sexy-and-cute outfit, which totally contradicted the chapters she had just written. Not only did the outfit say "I want you now", it said it with a dash of "and you cannot resist".

Beth arrived just as Riley cleaned up the last of her mess. She met her friend in the kitchen.

"He's coming for dessert, isn't he?"

Riley smiled. "Too obvious?"

"Not if you want some more of his magic." Beth pulled a bottle of Chardonnay from the bag of goodies she'd brought.

"Is that Thai I smell?" Riley's mouth watered.

Beth nodded. "I do get to stay long enough to say hi, don't I?"

Riley opened the wine and filled two glasses. "He'll be here at nine."

"So, we have lots of time to talk about last night." Beth took her wine glass and the bag of food into the living room.

Riley followed, choosing to sit on the floor Indian style, putting her at just the right height to eat with chopsticks. She had never been very good with chopsticks but loved Thai food.

"Basil Chicken?"

Beth pointed to the box and Riley dug in. After she'd had a few mouthfuls, she handed the box over to Beth in trade for the special Thai rice. She snagged a shrimp, savoring the garlic-ginger flavor.

"Okay. Enough food. Dish out the details, chick."

Riley sipped her wine around a huge smile. A light shiver snaked up her spine at the thought of Shane and the incredible night they had shared. "He's amazing. I would swear the man had taken Viagra because he was hard all night long." Riley licked her lips at the memory of his long, hard, satiny cock. "And he is huge!" Feeling guilty for kissing and telling, Riley held out her hands to demonstrate his length, then she used her thumb and middle finger to show his width.

Beth squirmed in her seat. "How the hell can you walk today?"

Riley laughed at her friend's' expression of shock and envy. "I don't know. I'm a little sore but I would jump him again in a second." Riley grabbed the Basil Chicken. She managed to keep both a piece a chicken and a Basil leaf captive with her chopsticks. "This is almost as good as sex. I love this stuff."

"So do I." Beth took the carton with one hand and shoved another at Riley. "Try the red curry eggplant and gimmey the chicken."

Riley dug into another of her favorites. They ate in silence for a few minutes. Finishing off the last of the food. Riley was full and happy. She took the empty cartons to the kitchen while Beth topped off their wine. "Do you think he has a friend?" Beth asked once they were settled on either end of the deep couch, facing one another.

"He mentioned one at Altitude." Riley frowned, "But honestly, I don't know. Come to think of it. I don't know much about him at all. We mainly talked about me last night and though it didn't occur to me until just now, he kind of avoided talking about himself."

Beth nudged Riley's foot. "Duh. He's a guy. They always avoid talking about themselves, unless they're like your brother, and then they have to brag about totally unimportant shit. You know -- the macho, egotistical, I have a bigger dick than you type of shit."

"Yeah. I guess so."

At Riley's faraway look, Beth said, "Hey, at least he was interested enough in you to ask questions. Most guys talk about themselves and don't care about you until it's time for the horizontal mambo." Beth took a drink, "My last date was proof of that. The guy actually expected me to put out just because he bought me dinner. What a fucking dinosaur."

Riley laughed. Beth always knew how to put a positive spin on things. "You've had your pick of a thousand men. When are you going to quit being the Sex-In-The-City-slut and settle down?"

"When I find the guy who can give me sixteen orgasms in one night."

That made Riley laugh from deep in her belly. When she got control of her voice, she said "You can't have Shane. Sorry. I love you, but I will fight you to the death if you go after him." Riley smiled as she spoke but a stab of fear nipped her heart.

Beth had landed several of the high school boys Riley had liked. Even in middle school, the boy Riley had a crush on had chosen Beth. It still hurt Riley that her friend always got the guy. Just once, Riley wanted the guy. She just hoped that the guy -- this specific guy--wanted her back.

Chapter Seven

S hane stopped by the Gym to check on things, then worked out for an hour. He couldn't stop thinking about Riley and wondered if he had really messed things up by sleeping with her. Not that it wasn't the most satisfying sex he had ever had, but he needed information from her to figure out why his parents had died.

The sex complicated things big time. Focus impossible around her. His military training should've allowed him to resist her. And yet, he'd called her already.

Made a date with her.

Already.

Shane climbed the short flight of stairs from the living room and headed down the hallway of his childhood home: built on the side of hill, with pine trees rising up the back slope. Technically, a three-story house, but only because of the hill. The living area and kitchen on the first level, then three bedrooms and two bathrooms on the second and finally a real flight of stairs went up to a loft area and a master suite.

He stopped in the doorway of the office where Nick pounded at a keyboard. "Anything new?"

Nick grinned. "Well, if it isn't Mr. Studley. How's it hanging? Or did it fall off after your all-nighter?"

"You shoulda been a comedian," Shane said dryly.

"Still may." Nick laughed. "And no. Nothing new."

"How's Katie?"

"Seems okay. She's been pretty quiet since breakfast."

Shane nodded and headed past his old bedroom to Katie's door. He knocked.

"Come in."

He went inside the still pink room, "Whaddya up to?" She set her book aside and looked up at him, the sadness in her eyes broke his heart.

"Reading." She sat up straighter and leaned against the white headboard.

"Feel like getting out of here and doing something?" Shane had no idea what to suggest, but he wanted his high energy, outgoing, brat of a sister back.

Katie shrugged. "Like what?"

"A movie. Ice skating. Lunch. Sledding."

Her mouth curved into a slow smile. "Ice skating? Really? You hate skating."

"Yeah. We'll drag Nick along too. He hates it more than me."

"Give me a few minutes." Katie jumped up from the bed. "The outdoor rink, right?"

"Sure. It's actually a mild day." Mild in Tahoe meant no wind and temperatures barely above freezing. "See you downstairs in a few minutes?"

"Yay! Yes." Katie's excited response made Shane smile.

He shared the bad news with Nick, who was less than thrilled since he hated ice skating. Shane laughed and went to his own room to change into appropriate clothing. As he stripped down to his boxer briefs, he thought of Riley, immediately regretting it as his dick hardened. He didn't understand the ease at which he got excited around her -- and apparently when he wasn't around her.

He pulled on cortex long johns, then his jeans, a ski shirt and his military issue fleece finished off his attire. He snagged his gloves and a beanie and went down to the kitchen to grab some water.

"I'm ready." Katie and Nick each took their own waters from the fridge and the trio headed for the garage.

Shane and Katie had their own skates. Luckily for Nick, or maybe not so much so, Shane had an older pair, which he handed his friend. "Gee, thanks." Nick took the skates and scowled.

Shane and Katie laughed.

The outdoor ice rink located in the Heavenly Village doubled as a miniature golf course in the summer months. People watched, the vibe upbeat and playful.

Shane only fell a few times, and he really didn't mind all that much because Katie laughed and played and seemed like her old self. She glided on the ice, did spins and other things that had names Shane couldn't remember. Nick skated better than he'd let on and he and Katie entertained onlookers with an impressive partner's routine. They skated well together.

A familiar tingling threaded up Shane's back. His gaze darted around the rink, landing on Trevor Stone. Shane's experience had proved that there was no such thing as coincidence. He pretended to retie his skates while keeping an eye on Riley's brother. He skated out to join Nick and Katie, grabbing each by the hand and making a circle. They automatically went into a spin together. The years of running missions with Nick resulted in unspoken rules between the two best friends.

Nick spotted Trevor.

Shane let go and Nick kept hold of Katie, guiding her toward the farthest rail. Shane joined then within seconds. "I've had enough, Katie. Can we go get some lunch?"

"Sure."

Protecting Katie's back, the two men followed her to a bench after stopping to retrieve their street shoes from a locker. Shane excused himself as soon as his shoes were on. "I need to use the restroom. I'll see you at the car."

By the time Katie and Nick got to the car, Shane had checked it over. He didn't find anything suspicious but his instincts were on high alert. Trevor's presence spooked him. And he sure as hell wasn't taking any chances where Katie's safety was concerned.

"What do you guys want to eat?" Shane asked as he climbed behind the wheel, all the while watching for signs of Trevor. He backed out of the parking space and slowly drove through the garage, scanning cars for suspicious activity or occupants.

Nick scanned the area as well, occasionally signaling Shane to check out a car or a single man walking leisurely. When they pulled into the sunlit street, Shane's tension eased.

"No suggestions for food?"

"I could go for a pizza," Nick said. "Pizza okay with you Katie?"

"Sure. Whatever you guys want."

Katie's voice held a note of sadness. Shane wondered if she had seen Trevor.

He looked into the rearview mirror and watched her expression. Distant. Scared.

Damn. Shane's insides tightened. He hated the haunted look in Katie's eyes. Hated that she had been witness to their parents' death. Hated the whole damned situation.

When he'd had to ring out of the SEALS program, the sense of failure and shame had been overwhelming; the worst nightmare of his life, until this. He had to fight to yank himself out of a spiraling sense of depression. Instead, he needed to get mad and get even.

He forced his voice to sound upbeat and cheerful. "Okay. Pizza it is. Primos?"

"Well, duh. It's only the best in town."

Shane smiled. Okay so maybe she wasn't as distant as Shane had thought. Her smart mouth still worked.

Shane checked the clock. He had agreed to meet Riley at nine. It was almost six. Maybe he should call her and cancel. His dick reminded him that he needed to see her.

Nick ordered the pizza while Shane and Katie chose a booth in the corner next to the arcade. Shane took a seat that allowed him a view of the front door.

"I'll be in the arcade. Call me when pizza's here." Katie dropped her coat on the seat next to Shane. "Some money, please." She held out her hand.

Shane dug into his pocket, pulled out a few crinkled single's. She snagged them and sauntered into the arcade just as Nick sat down.

"She had fun today." Nick took a long drink from his beer.

Shane could read his friend easily. Years of working side by side, covering each other in dangerous situations, killing to keep from being killed, bound them more than blood ties ever could. Tension curled itself around Nick like a snake squeezing the life out of its prey.

Shane watched the door. Nick watched the arcade. Without looking at his friend, Shane asked, "What?"

Nick shook his head, staring into the arcade. Shane wanted to turn around, but didn't. Nick inclined his head.

Trevor. How the hell did he get into the arcade? Then Shane remembered that it connected to the toy store. Panic seized his heart. Nick stood, went to the arcade entrance.

"Katie? Pizza."

A minute ticked by, to Shane it was an hour. That he had forgotten about the other entrance into the arcade disturbed him. His training taught him to examine every angle, predict every possible threat or scenario. How could he have made a mistake that could've cost his sister her life? Riley.

Then Katie came out and sat across from Shane. Relief swept through him. And guilt. Wanting Riley was dangerous. In more ways than one. He had made a mistake. He couldn't let it happen again.

Nick slid in next to Katie just as the pizza arrived. He nodded at Shane. Trevor was still there. For now.

"How'd you do?" Shane asked Katie as he served up a piece of pizza fully loaded with every meat in the joint, and a piece of Katie's favorite, pepperoni and pineapple.

"Not so good." Katie served herself, dumped a ton of crushed red pepper on her pizza and took a big bite.

Shane smiled. His sister had the appetite of a line-backer, but managed to stay slim and fit.

"So, did you spend the night with the redhead?" Shane almost choked on his pizza. "Do you think I'm stupid, dear brother? I know you didn't come home last night. I'm depressed, and sad, and feel guilty about living when Mom and Dad didn't, but I'm not stupid."

Dumbfounded, Shane stared at his baby sister, who was no longer a baby, obviously. His heart ached for her and yet he had never loved her more. The attitude was still there, lying low, but there nonetheless.

Shane and Katie had always been very close. While in the Navy and even when he went deep uncover for the DEA, he still managed to call home weekly. Katie always ran to phone, excited to hear the latest stories from her big brother.

"Well?" A smile tugged at the corner of her mouth. "I guess that's a yes? She's very pretty." Katie said without looking up from her plate.

"And it is about time for you to settle down and get married. You're getting old."

Nick laughed. "I guess that makes me ancient."

Shane ignored his friend and wondered how the hell to respond to Katie's comments. He'd gone after Riley to get to Trevor, but things weren't going quite the way he'd planned. He was hot for her. And it scared the hell out of him. She made him lose focus. He wanted her with an intensity like none he had ever experienced.

"Are you going to see her again?"

Shane nodded. "Supposed to see her at nine."

Chapter Eight

"I guess he's not coming." Riley yawned.

"It's only nine-twenty." Beth offered.

Riley felt the long-forgotten twang of disappointment. She hadn't spent much time in the dating scene but it only took one time to remember how much rejection sucked. Riley's first love -- a boy named Steve -- dumped her. Beth stole her high school crushes and then she caught her husband boinking the wanna-be-actress.

The disappointment burned like acid. And here it was again. She should have known that last night had been too good to be true. What she took for a real connection turned out to be simple male testosterone and horn dog behavior.

"He isn't coming." Riley gathered the empty wine glasses and headed for the kitchen. "I know it sounds cliché but he could've called. Then again, isn't the no call no show thing pretty popular among the male population?"

Beth followed her to the sink. Drying the glasses after Riley washed them. "They do lean toward complete insensitivity and an utter lack of consideration, don't they? But seriously, Rye. You have become so cynical since the divorce." Beth put the wine glasses in the cabinet. "They aren't all bad. Maybe something big came up and he hasn't been able to call. From what you said about last night, I don't believe it was just casual sex. Sixteen orgasms isn't the norm for a wham-bam-thank-you-ma'am one night stand."

"Twenty." Riley said as she held back a giggle.

Beth looked at her as though she'd truly lost it. "Twenty what?"

"Twenty orgasms. You said sixteen. It was twenty."

Beth smacked Riley with the dish towel. "Bragging doesn't become you."

Riley laughed, but she still looked at the clock. Nine thirty-five.

The phone rang. Riley stared at it.

"Answer the damn thing." Beth pushed Riley toward the counter where her phone sat.

"Hello?"

"Red. It's Shane." The husky tone brought visions of smoldering sex to Riley's mind, melting her anger. "I'm sorry I'm late." His voice grew huskier, "I'm heading your way armed with dessert."

Riley smiled, but she couldn't dismiss her earlier hurt and disappointment so easily. "It's getting late, Shane. I don't know if I'm still up for company." She looked at Beth whose shocked expression made her laugh aloud.

"Playing hard to get again, are you?" Shane lowered his voice. "I promise to make you pay."

Riley's vagina clenched. "I suppose I can give you a chance at redemption."

Now Shane laughed. "Good. See you in five."

Riley hung up. "He'll be here in five minutes." She ran through the house, picking up random things, straightening pillows.

She felt Beth's gaze and turned to see her friend leaning against the wall between the kitchen and living room. Amusement danced in her expression. "Can't wait to watch the two of you squirm while awaiting my departure." Beth sauntered to the couch and plopped down, grabbing a freshly fluffed pillow and hugging it close. "Beats the hell out of late-night TV."

"You wouldn't dare." Riley frowned.

Beth grinned. "Fifteen minutes, max. Then I'm gone."

"Pinky swear?"

"Pinky swear." The women locked pinkies, cinching the deal.

A car door slammed and then the sound of footsteps trudging up the outer stairs.

Riley smoothed, or tried to smooth her hair. She did a quick finger under each eye to catch any melted mascara and opened the door.

Shane grabbed her before she realized what was happening. His lips seared hers, hot and demanding. When she felt his tongue probing for entry, she parted her lips. He tasted of mint and smelled like pine and man. Riley moaned, then, realizing they had an audience, pulled away from his embrace.

"That was a hell-of-a-hello, but we have company." Riley stepped aside, closing the door. Shane kicked off his wet boots, handed Riley a grocery bag and shed his coat.

His smile held no shame. "Hi, Beth."

"Hello, Shane," Beth threw the pillow aside. "Great to see you again."

Riley went into the kitchen. She reached into the bag tentatively. The first thing she pulled out was a box of giant chocolate covered strawberries. Next a bottle of champagne. The last two items caught her so off guard that she broke into a bout of laughter. Shane came into the kitchen, clearly entertained by her shock.

Beth stood behind him, her eyebrows inched upward, a frown on her face. "What's so funny?"

Riley dropped the toys into the bag, "Nothing. Just an inside joke."

Beth's frown deepened, then she forced a smile. "Okay. I get the hint. I'm out of here. You guys have fun." She gave Riley a quick hug. "I'll talk to you in the morning."

"Not too early." Riley and Shane answered in unison.

Riley's tummy did a tilt-o-whirl drop and they all laughed.

"Got it." Beth gathered her coat and slipped quietly downstairs and into the garage.

The door clanked upward, then down as Beth's tail lights flickered out of sight.

Riley poked Shane in the chest. "You got some 'splainin to do."

Shane snatched her finger in his grip. "Later." He pulled her to him and picked up where their earlier kiss left off. Riley moaned as his tongue danced with hers. He backed her against the kitchen counter, lifted her up. "Nice jammies, but I am afraid they have to go." In one swift motion, Shane had her pants off and her butt safely on the cold tile counter. She lifted her arms as he dragged her top upward. "Much better." Shane's eyes darkened as he stared at her exposed breasts.

The fire inside Riley ignited when his lips touched her nipple. He sucked and pulled and she thought she would die from the sheer pleasure of it. Then he switched to the other as his hand found her wet and throbbing center. "Mm." He moaned as he teased her clitoris.

Riley pulled at his t-shirt, wanting to feel his smooth skin and hard muscle. He broke contact with her breast and dripping pussy just long enough to get his shirt off, then he was right back at it and Riley felt the tightening within her.

Shane sensed her readiness and entered her slippery canal with first one finger, then a second. Riley gasped as the coil tightened. She leaned back, letting go of her need to touch Shane in favor of the explosion she felt would rock her at any moment. She closed her eyes as Shane used one hand to rub her clit in a circular motion that coincided with the fingers inside her. "Oh. My. God." Riley's body convulsed as her orgasm ripped through her. Shane continued to draw every last sensation out of her as he found her lips and kissed her hard.

When he withdrew and stepped back a fist tightened around his heart. Riley looked beautiful as she opened her eyes and sighed, pulling herself back from what had been an earthshaking orgasm. The raw need to please her shocked him. The knowledge that he had given her such intense pleasure rocked his world off its axis. For the first time in his life, Shane was truly terrified. Guns and bombs didn't hold nearly as much power to scare him as his feelings for Riley did.

"Turnabout, buddy." She purred as she slowly slid down from the counter.

She reached for his fly, unbuttoned, unzipped and then pushed his pants and boxers down. As his hardness popped up, she sucked it into her mouth, shocking his senses. He thought he would come right then, but struggled to maintain a degree of control because it felt so damned good. She licked the length of him as he stepped out of his jeans. She sucked at him as she pulled a sock from each foot. When she stood, he sighed, wanting her hot mouth wrapped around him again.

"On the counter." She said with a wicked grin. He obeyed. Riley bent to take him back into her mouth. He threaded his fingers in her hair as he fed her his cock. She drew it slowly into the back of her throat as she softly kneaded his balls.

Riley looked up and met his eyes. He groaned at the sight of her sucking his big dick all the way to the base. "You need...to...stop...or," he gave her a gentle nudge, "I'm going to come."

A smile lit her eyes as he eased his cock from her warm, wet mouth. Jumping from the counter, Shane rolled a condom down his hard length.

He lifted Riley, impaling her. She screamed, her eyes filled with a surprise that quickly turned to pleasure as he rammed in and out, in and out. She kissed his neck and shoulders and the coiling of another orgasm had her clutching at him.

Shane slowed his pace, wanting to draw her out.

"Faster, Shane."

He chuckled. "Greedy, aren't we?"

"Please."

He reached down, his finger finding her clit as he continued his sweet torture. The contact sent her over the edge. As soon as she clenched around him, he let go. His body tensed as he shot a hot load of come into the condom that he really wished he wasn't wearing.

He wanted to feel Riley completely.

He rested his head on the wall beside her head until he caught his breath.

She continued clutching at his cock. "That was soooo nice," she said in a breathless whisper.

"Yeah. Pretty amazing." He answered, then kissed her as he slowly pulled out. He set her down. "I could use some water and a seat. How about you?"

Riley took champagne flutes from the cabinet and set them on the counter. "I have just the ticket. You get the drinks. I'll start the bath."

"Bath?" He was in deep trouble.

She gave him a sultry smile. "Uh huh. Through the living room, down the hall and to the right. Can't miss it." She patted his butt on the way past him.

Feisty little vixen on top of sexy and intelligent and really hot and... *You have got to get a grip, man. She will kill you at this rate.*

Shane pulled open the refrigerator door, poured champagne into the flutes on the counter, grabbed the strawberries and his bag of tricks.

He peeked at her bed as he passed it. Warm and inviting, just as he suspected. He continued to the right.

"Nice," he said as he turned the corner into an amazing bathroom.

Seeing Riley, naked and bent over the partially sunken Jacuzzi tub was a hell of a sight too, and it woke his dick up like a quadruple shot of espresso. He set down the treats he'd brought on a foot-wide counter that surrounded the back section of the tub.

Riley turned and smiled. "Care to join me?" She didn't wait for an answer. She climbed into the bubble filled water.

"What do you think?" He asked with a glance at his ever-hardening member.

"I think you'd love to."

He laughed out loud. "You'd be right," he said as he joined her in the citrus-scented tub.

Riley sprawled on the bed her legs tangled in Shane's. "I think your toys will have to wait. I can't take any more." Riley snuggled close to Shane in her comfy four-poster feather bed.

"I suppose I can use a rest too." He pulled her closer. "So how long have known Beth?"

"Most of my life. I can't remember not knowing her."

Shane rubbed Riley's arm. "Is she involved with anyone?"

Riley's old fears sliced through her at Shane's question. She pushed them aside. "No. She isn't very good at dating. Her expectations are way too high."

"Maybe she just hasn't met the right guy. We should introduce her to my friend, Nick. I can't remember the last time he had a date. What do you think about dinner at my place, tomorrow night?"

As deep as he was sinking, he needed Nick to help him get dirt on Trevor.

Last night he planted a listening device in Riley's cell phone. Trevor called her earlier today but Riley hadn't answered and Trevor hadn't left any messages.

"You thirsty?" Shane asked.

"Parched."

Shane untangled himself from the warmth of Riley's luscious body. "Two cold waters coming up."

Shane stopped on his way to the kitchen to retrieve a listening device from the pocket of the pants he had discarded earlier. He quickly placed the tiny chip in the cordless phone, then grabbed two bottles of water from the fridge.

Guilt caused Shane to stop on his way back to the bedroom. Why not just ask Riley about her relationship with Trevor? He struggled with the idea as he tried to shake off the guilt niggling at him.

Riley leaned against the headboard with the comforter tucked under her arms. The way her auburn hair fanned out against the pillow, combined with the sleepy look in her eyes had Shane's cock pulsing. He leaned down and kissed her on the forehead before handing her the water.

She smiled. "Dinner tomorrow sounds like a wonderful idea. I'll call Beth in the morning."

Shane climbed in beside Riley and drew her close. "So, do you have any other siblings?"

"No. Just Trevor and I."

"You and Trevor didn't seem to be happy to see each other the other night. What's his story?"

"It's a long story," Riley said as she sank down into his embrace. "I'm too tired to tell you my childhood woes. Suffice it to say that Trevor has his own way of thinking about things. The world owes him something for some reason that no one, including Trevor can explain," her voice lowered as sleep tried to takes its hold. "Sometimes I almost feel sorry for him."

Shane lay awake long after Riley fell asleep. Clearly, Riley and Trevor weren't close. She might not even know enough to help Shane and though he thought planting bugs a waste, he needed to follow through. He eased his way from the bed without waking Riley.

With a heavy heart, Shane tiptoed up the stairs. Moonlight slipped through the wall of glass in Riley's office allowing Shane to soak in the details of the large office. Plants cast shadows along the walls, one of which boasted descending shelves filled with books. The A-framed room felt warm even in the darkness of the winter night.

Shane planted a small listening device under the outer edge of the cherry wood table. He couldn't help but glance at the scribbled pages scattered on top of the table, beside a lap top.

A downright dirty sex scene, reminiscent of last night had Shane's dick twitching to attention. He dropped into the soft leather chair and dropped his head in his hands. What the hell was he doing? He should just ask Riley outright what kind of relationship her brother had with Domino.

Frustrated, Shane eased down the stairs, and made his way quietly back to bed. Riley mumbled as he pulled her closer. When her breathing slowed and evened out, Shane closed his eyes and tried to push down his guilt.

Chapter Nine

S hane kissed Riley goodbye after a delicious breakfast in bed. He felt like a schmuck. He was falling hard for her. The idea that he had violated her privacy gnawed at him, but he had to find the guy responsible for his parents' death, and not just for vengeance. Katie would never be safe until the killer was tried and convicted. He would find a way to make Riley understand his betrayal.

Somehow.

He spent the day at the gym, doing the books, working out. He interviewed eight people for the job of manager. No matter how the investigation into his parents' death ended, Shane couldn't manage the gym. He was committed to the DEA for the next few years. Working out of San Francisco for the Organized Crime Task Force meant he could be reassigned in a heartbeat.

Nick's contacts and the fact that the local Tahoe authorities had a hard-on for Domino were the reasons Shane had gotten lucky and pulled the e-ticket to Tahoe.

He couldn't -- wouldn't -- lose sight of that reality. No matter what happened with Riley, he would have no choice but to move on to another location, another assignment.

He stirred the spaghetti sauce again, then smeared a light coat of butter on the sourdough loaf, sprinkled it with garlic seasoning, basil and parmesan.

For the last hour, Shane had watched Nick hack into Domino's computer systems. So far, they hadn't found any links to Trevor, but they had found some interesting ties to one of the employees at Domino's restaurant who had previously worked at the gym.

Finally, a lead. Somewhere to start.

Dominico's Italian Restaurant and The Basement were both legitimate businesses but they both provided Domino with a front to run his illegitimate business; running drugs and laundering money.

"Smells good." Nick poured a glass of wine from the open bottle of Merlot on the counter. He had showered while Shane finished up the last-minute dinner preparations. "How long has Beth known Riley?"

"Since grade school. I'm guessing Beth will have a few interesting stories about Trevor. The way she looked at him at the club the other night suggests she really hates the guy."

Shane checked the clock. Twenty minutes. His pulse quickened. He really couldn't wait to see Riley. He turned the gas on beneath the large pasta pan.

"What's Katie up to?" Shane took a sip of his wine to hide his smile as he watched Nick pace the narrow length of kitchen. His friend was nervous.

"She's changing into 'appropriate dinner attire'."

Shane laughed at his friend's attempt to mimic Katie. "Mom was big on etiquette."

"Whatever." Nick took a long swallow of his wine.

"Your mom must've taught you the same lessons." Shane said with a grin. His friend wore jeans and a light blue button-down shirt, which matched his icy blue eyes. The fabric looked soft and expensive.

Unable to resist, Shane continued. "Or are you hoping to impress Beth and get lucky?"

"Fuck off, Shane."

The doorbell chimed, suddenly Shane's nerves kicked in. How would he keep his hands off of Riley for the next few hours? More importantly, would Katie like her?

"I'll get it," Nick offered.

Shane opened another bottle of Merlot and poured two glasses as he listened to the introductions in the hallway. When Riley entered the kitchen, his stomach flipped and his dick twitched. She was dressed in a pair of jeans that accented her luscious curves, but it was the dark purple sweater hugging her body and exposing the creamy mounds of her beautiful breasts that did him in. He growled and moved toward her, "You look good enough to eat." He pulled her close, kissing her deeply. Releasing her, he hissed. "You make me crazy, woman."

"Thanks, I think." But she smiled.

"Oh, that was definitely a compliment. Wine?" he asked as he lifted a glass from the counter.

"Yes, thank you. Something smells wonderful." Riley moved through the kitchen, admiring the granite counters, the center island with pots hanging above it, the dining area that was more like a great room. "This is amazing. I've wanted to do something like this to my kitchen but the space is too small."

"This was my mother's favorite room. It's too bad it's dark outside because the view out those windows is pretty spectacular." Shane took her hand. "Come on, I'll show you the rest of the place."

Before they could get further than the living room, Shane's sister appeared. Shane made formal introductions and Riley extended her hand.

"It's a pleasure to meet you, Katie."

Katie looked Riley up and down. "Your sweater is beautiful." The words were so soft, Riley wasn't sure Katie had actually spoken aloud.

"Thank you."

"I'm glad Shane met you. He needs a girlfriend."

Riley darted a shocked look in Shane's direction. He laughed, as did Nick and Beth.

Shocked into silence, Riley simply stared.

Shane touched her waist with enough pressure to move Riley forward. "Shall we?"

After seeing an office, two bathrooms and three other bedrooms, Shane took her up a narrow staircase into a master suite, recently remodeled based on the fresh paint scent and chic masculine décor. Riley assumed this was the room Shane's parents had shared, but now it looked all Shane. Hard lines and deep textures. The blues and browns commingled well and gave the room a strong, comfortable feel.

A flat screen TV smaller than the one in the living room was mounted over the dark wood dresser. On the other wall, windows looked out at a snowy forest, barely visible in the moonlight.

"And this is my room." He took her wine glass and set it on the dresser, then grabbed her and yanked her against his hard body.

She hugged him close, loving the feel of his hard muscles against her small hands and soft breasts.

"I missed you today." He rubbed his hands over her shoulders, down her back, finally cupping her ass cheeks. "I want you so bad right now. I thought I could handle it, but I can't."

Riley laughed. "You're incorrigible." But she stood on her tiptoes and met him for a kiss. It started out slow and sweet but quickly turned hungry and demanding until Shane broke contact. He led her hand to the bulge in his pants. "This is what you do to me."

Riley had never considered herself overly sexual or aggressive but she felt like such a temptress by Shane's bold and honest desire. She ran her hands lightly over her chest, down her stomach and to the button of her jeans, watching Shane as his eyes followed her hands. She shimmied her jeans down, reached into her panties and then held her damp finger out to Shane. "And this is what you do to me."

Thank the Lord they were upstairs, Shane thought as he closed the bedroom door. With lightening-speed he had Riley's finger in his mouth. His hands consumed her. Her clothes came off so fast she wondered if they had evaporated.

"Sorry, sweet thing, but I can't wait." Shane lifted her onto his huge erection, sheathed in a condom and started pumping her up and down.

She held onto to his shoulders and watched the passion and pleasure dance in his eyes. With one hand he supported her while the other reached between them and found her most sensitive spot.

"I want you to come for me. Now." He rubbed her clit with his thumb, bringing her to a gushing orgasm just as he released his own.

When their breathing stabilized, he separated them and set her down. She kissed him softly before gathering her clothes. "I'll just freshen up and be right back."

Shane gave her a few minutes, then joined her in the bathroom. "Sorry about that," he said as he kissed the back of her neck.

She met his gaze in the mirror. "Don't be sorry. I started it. Sort of."

"Oh yeah. You did. Talk about incorrigible." He swatted her butt. "We better go tend to dinner."

Riley smoothed her hair, smiling as she followed Shane back to the kitchen. She really liked him. Tons. Megatons. Enormously. And it wasn't just about the sex. Of course, the sex was stellar, but there was something about him that spoke to her heart. Her Soul. The emotion she sometimes saw flash across his face when he thought she wasn't looking. The way his grin made her stomach flip.

They worked side-by-side in the kitchen putting the finishing touches on what turned out to be a wonderful dinner. The Caesar salad was superb, the spaghetti even better. The dinner conversation never wavered and Riley was fascinated with Katie. She and Shane had such an easygoing relationship and Riley envied the closeness they shared. He obviously cared very deeply for his little sister.

Trevor had never been the kind of big brother that Shane obviously was to Katie. Trevor had been bossy, cruel, and downright condemning. He always wanted to be center stage, criticizing Riley for being fat, or ugly, or stupid. And Riley had believed it. To some extent, she still did. Or had, until she met Shane. When once she was terrified to be seen naked in daylight, she now felt sexy. Thanks to Shane. In some ways it made her resent Trevor even more. But mostly, it made her appreciate Shane, and feel for him in ways that she had never felt before.

Terrified was at the top of her list. Well, no. It was second on her list. Lustful and horny as hell, a perpetual state of being since she had met Shane, was at the top of the list.

As if reading her mind, he winked at her from the kitchen doorway as he entered the dining room with a sinful looking cake.

"Shane!" Katie jumped from her chair and ran to him. "You didn't?"

His smile was wicked. "Didn't what, sis?"

Katie smacked him on the shoulder. He bent, feigning a slip of his grip. Katie grabbed for the tray, trying to right it. "Noooo!"

Shane laughed. A full, from the gut, happy laugh. "I did. And I would never drop your all-time favorite chocolate orgasmic cheesecake that mom used to make and that I found her recipe for."

Katie giggled.

"Thank you, Shane." Katie swiped at the tear dripping down her cheek.

To lighten the mood, Shane swatted at his sister. "I didn't make this for you. I have a lady to impress." His smiled belied his words.

Katie looked at Riley, "And I thought he went to all this trouble to take my mind off of my problems." She gave Shane the ultimate of teenaged attitude. Stink eye. "I should've known."

But Riley could clearly see that the siblings were teasing, and enjoying every second.

While forcing herself to eat a thin slice of the famous cheesecake, Riley decided that she really, really liked Shane Blackstone.

Really.

But she couldn't decide if she liked him more than the amazing cheesecake. The chocolate and orange flavors mixed with the creamy texture provided a plethora of flavor. Riley savored every scrumptious bite.

"I think my stomach is about to explode," Beth announced from her seat across the table.

Everyone laughed as Riley stood to clear away the dessert dishes.

"Don't," Nick said. "I'll clean up. After that meal, I need to move around."

"Me too," Beth smiled and winked at Riley.

Shane grabbed Riley's hand. "Sounds good to me. Let's go relax."

Riley sank into the soft, cozy couch. Katie changed the music to something a bit more energetic than Riley preferred, but still she closed her eyes and leaned against Shane.

Nick was delightful in a serious nerdy kind of way, but Riley hadn't overlooked his intense masculinity and obvious attraction to Beth. It made her smile, knowing that her friend might find the same crazy passion Riley enjoyed, because Beth was very clearly attracted to Nick too.

And Katie? She was delightful in a wounded soaking-up-every-last-ounce-of-attention kind of way. Riley could relate to her on so many levels. She had always felt out of place. Her brother had made her feel fat and ugly all through her childhood. And mostly she *was* kind of frumpy. Overweight and pimply and then just overweight. And the girls at Covington had only reinforced that.

But Katie was a beautiful young woman. Long blonde hair with just the right amount of curl, gorgeous blue-green eyes, a small waist and very generous breasts. She had no reason to feel shy and insecure, except for maybe the fact that her parents had been murdered. That was probably a much better reason to be withdrawn and tentative than any Riley could think of.

"I'm about to fall asleep," Shane complained. "We need to do something to get my blood pumping or I'm afraid I'll have to call it a night."

"Shane!" Katie had a look of appalled shock on her face.

Shane looked confused, then realization dawned and he actually blushed.

"No. I didn't mean...I was thinking we should play a board game or go for a walk."

Nick and Beth laughed.

"Oh." Katie blushed a darker shade of red than Shane had. Katie went to the built-in shelves and scanned a stack of games. "Yahtzee?"

Before anyone could answer, Riley's cell phone chimed a soothing Zen melody. "Excuse me," Riley said as she stood and went to the front entry to retrieve her phone from her purse.

The display indicated the caller was her brother. He had called her three times in the last two days. Riley found that very odd, especially since he had only wanted to tell her to stay away from Shane, but she longed for something like what Shane and Katie shared, so Riley took a huge leap and answered the phone.

"Hey, Trev. What's up?" She tried to sound cheerful.

"What the fuck are you doing with Blackstone?" Trevor's vulgar question caught her so off guard that Riley actually stumbled into the entry table, nearly knocking it over. Shane was there in an instant, a concerned look creasing his brow.

"I'm sorry?" Riley was too stunned to say much more.

"I know where you are. What the hell are you doing with him?" Her brother had always been distant and mean, but this was so extreme and so...weird. He sounded like a maniac.

"Trevor, have you been drinking?" Riley didn't know what else to say. His behavior was bizarre. More so than usual anyway. "I don't know what your problem is--"

"You need to stay away from him. Go home. Now. Or you'll get caught in the crossfire."

"What are you talking about, Trevor? You aren't making any sense." Riley shrugged as Shane watched her. Closely. "And how did you know where I was?"

Shane took the phone from her. "Do you have a problem that I should know about...Trev?" The venomous tone surprised Riley. On so many levels.

She fell against the wall. How had her brother known where she was? Why was he so violently opposed to her being with Shane? Why would he know she was with Shane? And why had Shane grabbed the phone? What the hell was going on?

Beth appeared. A beacon in a storm. She pushed Shane aside. "I got this."

Riley watched Shane go into the living room, albeit tentatively.

Beth took her hand, pulling her into the kitchen for some privacy. "What the hell just happened?"

Riley shook her head. "I don't know. Trevor called asking questions about why I was with Shane. Told me to stay away from him or I would be caught in the crossfire."

"But how did he--"

"Know I was here?" Riley shivered, crossing her arms across her chest.

Before she could even consider an answer, Shane, Nick and Katie were in the kitchen.

Riley looked at each of them, feeling like a total fool. It wasn't really a big deal. Okay, so maybe having your brother threaten you, or worse, stalk you for no fathomable reason was cause for alarm. "I'm okay, really. Just surprised. Why would Trevor tell me to stay away from you?" She directed her question at Shane.

"He actually told you to stay away from me?" Shane ran a hand through his hair.

"Yeah. He told me that I might get caught in the crossfire. What the hell is that supposed to mean? Didn't you just meet Trevor the other night?"

"Trevor?" Katie's question was barely audible.

Riley watched the color drain from her pretty face. "Yes. He's my brother. Do you..."

Riley didn't finish her question. Katie grasped her head in her hands as she sunk to the floor. She started rocking, a crazy humming, whining sound rent the air, bringing the hairs on Riley's arms and back standing straighter than a flag pole.

Shane dropped to the floor, embracing his sister. "It's okay Katie. You're okay." Shane rocked his sister until she quieted.

"I'll get Katie settled." Nick put a hand on Shane's shoulder. "Call Dr. Banks."

Shane watched as Nick carried Katie from the room, wondering how he would explain this situation, and how Trevor knew that they were onto him.

But most of all, he wondered whether or not Katie was finally starting to remember. If so, Trevor most certainly was involved, because Katie's reaction to his name couldn't have been coincidental.

Shane wanted Katie to remember more than anything. If Katie remembered who killed their parents, Shane could find justice, maybe even peace. Maybe he could finally settle down. He reached into his pocket and dialed the all too familiar number for Dr. Banks.

Riley stood beside Beth her arms crossed over her chest to ward off the chill easing up her spine. Trevor sounded crazy, but Riley suspected there was some truth to his rambling. Shane had gone pale when he heard Trevor's accusation. And Katie had withdrawn like a frightened child at the mention of Trevor's name.

Shane turned to Riley as he put his cell phone back into his pocket. "We need to talk." His focus on Beth when he spoke.

"Gotcha." Beth said quietly. "I'll be in the next room if you need me." She squeezed Riley's arms before she faced Shane.

"I'll get the story from Nick, so don't leave anything out."

Shane only nodded.

When Beth was gone, Shane pulled out a chair and motioned for Riley to sit. A sinking feeling wrapped around her heart. Shane settled in the chair across from her. He reached for her hand, then looked into her eyes. She saw the sadness clouding them.

"My parents were killed in an accident a while back and Katie was involved." He looked down at their intertwined hands, "My parents had been out to dinner. Katie was home alone. She freaked out over some noises outside, said she saw someone peeking in the windows, and called Dad. They came home. Katie opened the front door just as they were pulling into the driveway. They always came in through the garage but she was too scared to wait. Dad climbed from the car," Shane stopped, sucked in a calming breath. "An explosion knocked him clear across the street. My Mother..." Shane released Riley's hands and stood, "was blown to bits. Katie watched it all. She suffered minors cuts and burns from the shrapnel."

Shane ran a hand through his hair. He paced the kitchen like a caged animal, finally settling down in a chair across from Riley.

Riley wanted to go to him, but couldn't. She knew there was more. And she sensed she wasn't going to like it.

"My Dad had been trying to get proof that a man named Domino was trafficking drugs through his restaurant. He also runs a club called *The Basement*. It's a rave club where he pushes his street drugs, but more importantly, where he uses the latest date rape drug on the girls who attend the raves."

Riley shivered. "Oh my God. Trevor works at The Basement. He's a bouncer there."

"Exactly."

Shane was staring at Riley now, watching as the gears clicked into place. Shock warred with something Shane couldn't identify. She wouldn't look at him, but stared at her hands as she rubbed them together.

"It was supposed to be a way to get close to Trevor, but when I saw you, touched you, it became..."

Tears clouded Riley's eyes.

"Shit." Shane hated to see a woman cry. He hated that he caused this. He knew the second he'd slept with her that he'd made a mistake. But he couldn't resist.

Shane stood again.

"I'm so sorry..." He rounded the table and pulled her into his arms. She tried to fight him, tried to push away, but he wouldn't let her run from him. He had to make her understand. "Please don't cry."

He couldn't stand knowing that he had hurt her so badly. The second he'd realized he was falling for Red he'd wanted to tell her the truth so that this wouldn't happen. His guts rumbled at the very thought that she would leave and never look back. He didn't think he could take the loss, the...

"I'm sorry," she whispered. Sniffling into his shoulder.

The words cut through Shane like a fillet knife. "What?"

He loosened his hold on her enough to lean back and look down into her eyes. "Sorry?" Why the hell would she apologize to him? "For what?"

"For what happened to your family. For what my brother has done." Riley reached up and touched his face. "I'm so sorry."

Shane couldn't have been more surprised. He laid his hand over hers. "You're amazing." He leaned down and brushed a soft kiss across her lips, then wrapped his arms around her. His eyes filling with tears, he squeezed them shut as he inhaled the sweet clean scent that he had come to know so well.

When he released her, Riley pointed a finger at him and started poking him in the chest. "Don't think I'm not pissed at your deception, Shane. I am. I was betrayed by my ex-husband, and trust doesn't come easily to me. You betrayed me by not telling me the truth from the start. If I didn't understand your reasons, if I didn't know my brother as well as I do, I would leave...I'm still thinking about it." He backed away from her, trying to keep from smiling. Her anger, though gently directed at him, made him adore and respect her more than he already did. "But I believe you, because I'm in love with you and because I can easily believe my brother is involved in this too. I would've helped you from the start if you had asked."

Shane grabbed her hands and drew her up against him. "What did you say?"

"I said I believe my brother is involved."

"No, before that."

She looked confused.

"The part about loving me."

Riley gasped. "Did I say that out loud?"

Shane smiled. "Yeah. You did."

"Oh." Riley tried to look away. It was way too soon to declare the depth of her feelings for him. They had so much to learn about each other. But she did love him. She'd known from the moment he'd touched her.

You loved Robert too and look where that got you.

She shushed herself and waited, his silence killing her breath by slow breath.

She looked up and saw his smile. Heat leaped into her center, spreading like wildfire. He leaned down and kissed her with a possessiveness she had only read about in romance novels. The kind that made the heroine's knees weak and toes curl.

She wrapped her arms around Shane's neck and pressed her body against the hard plain of his chest. She loved the way he felt, the way they fit together.

The sound of the doorbell snapped Riley out of her mindless, sensual stupor.

"That would be the doc."

Chapter Ten

S hane paced the entire hour Dr. Banks spent with Katie. He thought he'd go flipping crazy. It was worse than any sensory deprivation exercise he suffered through during his training.

Having Riley by his side somehow made everything easier. He was still in shock she had so easily forgiven him for his deception. Still awed by her declaration of love.

His heart ached at the knowledge that she was his. He was both elated and terrified at what lay ahead for them and wanted nothing more than to declare his love in return and show her just how much a man could love a woman.

Riley and Beth were on the couch, huddled close and whispering. Shane felt their gazes lock on him, felt Riley's heated stare.

"What?" He said, finally turning and staring them down. "You two have been scheming. Let's have it."

Riley smiled, while Beth tried her best 'Who me?'.

"I can torture you until you talk." He glared at Riley, smiled at the flash of heat in her eyes as her face flushed. "In ways you have never dreamed of."

She squirmed.

Beth laughed out loud. "Get a room."

Shane grinned, but quickly turned serious at the sound behind him. Nick headed toward them his expression tight. Shane struggled to control his impatience.

Nick nodded toward the kitchen and Shane fell in line behind his friend. Once behind the closed door, Nick dropped into a chair. Shane waited, his fists tightening in frustration.

"Katie has shut down again. Dr. Banks thinks we should get her to a hospital where she can be under 24-hour observation. She said that..."

"No fucking way. We can't protect her." Shane headed for the door, ready to give the doctor a piece of his mind, but Nick was there, in front of him, blocking the exit.

"Shane, be reasonable. I'll call for back up and put two men on her door 24/7. She'll be fine. We have a better shot at catching these fuckers with Katie safely tucked away."

Shane stared into Nick's eyes. Anger and frustration raged through him, but his friend was right. Katie would be safer in the long run. At least she'd better be.

"Okay. How do we get her there?" Shane asked as he ran a hand through his hair.

"Beth." Nick answered.

"Beth?"

"Yeah. Her coloring and build are pretty close to Katie's. We use her as a decoy while I take Katie to Incline."

"Incline?"

"There's a very private and very exclusive rehab center there and Dr. Banks has access to a condo close by that in no way can be traced to her. She'll be able to spend a great deal of time with Katie and we can keep her safe."

Shane nodded. Nick seemed to have everything covered already. He should be relieved but he was too nervous. He didn't have just Katie to protect now, he also had to consider Riley. Her own brother had just threatened her. The bastard would pay one way or another.

"Let's fill the ladies in and get this thing going before I change my mind." Shane pushed through the door into the living room.

Riley stood, cautiously moved toward him. "You okay?"

Shane pulled her into him arms. "I will be. Thanks again for being so understanding." He kissed her soundly. "Nick has a plan for getting Katie away safely. We need your help." Shane turned to Beth.

"My help?" Confusion danced across her face. "I mean, sure. Whatever I can do, but what can I do?"

"Be Katie for a day." Nick sat beside her on the couch and explained his plan to whisk Katie away.

"I'm beat." Riley said as she climbed the stairs from her garage into the main living area.

"Me too." Shane was drained. It had been hard to watch Katie leave with Nick.

"You're welcome to stay here tonight," Riley dropped onto the couch.

"Are you sure?" Shane didn't think he could stay awake to drive home. It was four in the morning and though he would do it if he had to, he definitely didn't want to.

"Yes. I'm positive." Riley snuggled close to him. "This was hard for you, wasn't it?"

"It kills me to see Katie in so much pain. I don't want to go back to that empty house." He put his arm over her shoulder and pulled her closer. Then he leaned down and kissed her, reveling in the heat that crept into his blood. He shifted on the couch, pulling her on top of him as he eased back. He held her tight, deepened the kiss, finally releasing her when she groaned with obvious desire.

"I really am sorry, Riley."

She pulled back. "I know." She scooted backward, turning her body so she sat sideways. "I'm not sure I'm as okay with what you did as I may seem. I'm angry and I'm hurt."

"When Nick and I discovered you were Trevor's sister, we figured you were our best chance at getting close to him. I had no idea how estranged the two of you were until tonight."

"He called the morning after we met. His attitude in the bar didn't compare to the venom of the next morning." She picked up a pillow and hugged it close to her body. "He told me to stay away from you, that you were trouble. I should've asked you why he'd feel that way, maybe then you'd have talked to me."

The hopeful look in her eyes tugged at Shane's conscience. He wouldn't lie to her. "I probably wouldn't have told you the truth at that point."

Sadness filled her eyes.

"I guess I should come clean about everything."

"That would be smart."

"I planted a couple of listening devices in your home."

Fire shot into her eyes. She dropped the pillow and left the couch. He had to give her credit for her composure. She didn't yell and scream and pitch a fit.

"Where?"

Shane stood. He walked around the house, Riley on his heels, removing the bugs. He dropped them into her hand.

"Are there cameras too?"

Her tone unreadable, Shane decided against the flippant remark about wishing he had so he could watch her changing at night or showering, or maybe even touching herself while thinking of him. He couldn't help his thoughts so he answered simply, "No."

She handed the bugs to him. "Get these out of here, please."

Shane dropped them into his pocket. "I guess I should go and leave you to decide if you ever want to see me again."

Riley stood very still. "No. Don't go."

Stunned, he moved toward her. "If I stay, I won't be able to keep my hands off of you."

Her eyes smoldered with passion and something that Shane couldn't identify. "I wouldn't want you to. Maybe we should see how we do at make-up sex. Perhaps it will sway my final decision on whether or not I'll forgive you."

He smiled. "That's a great idea."

Riley led him to her room. When he reached up to unbutton his shirt, she slapped his hands away. "Please, let me."

Shane dropped his hands to his sides as she slowly undid the top button of his shirt.

"Sorry about that. I'm the one who needs forgiving."

Riley only smiled. She moved slowly down his shirt front. When she reached the bottom, she put her soft hands on his chest and spread the shirt over his shoulders, and down his arms. His cock throbbed, aching as his jeans tightened over it. She didn't undo the buttons at his wrists so when the shirt reached them, it stopped, confining him.

"Maybe I plan to punish you for such bad behavior." She smiled wickedly as she undid his jeans. Pulling them over his hips and letting them fall to his ankles. "You're excited, aren't you?"

"Yes."

She giggled and reached a finger into each side of the waist of his boxer briefs. She lowered herself as she lowered the boxers and when his long, thick erection sprang free, she snagged it into her mouth.

Shane gasped at the sheer pleasure of her hot mouth as it sucked and tugged at his pulsing cock. He was trapped. He couldn't use his hands, couldn't move his feet.

Riley reached around and grasped his buttocks, a hand on each cheek, flexing as she sucked his ever-hardening cock. "You're killing me here, Riley."

"Uh huh." She murmured. Then she opened her throat and took him fully into her mouth, released him, pulled him back in. He was going to come. No doubt, very soon. And she seemed to know it. She reached under his shaft and fondled his hardened testicles. Then, she slid a finger toward his anus. The pleasure was too intense. Shane reached his hands behind his back and ripped his shirt from his wrists. He grabbed her head, ran his fingers through her hair, pulling to release the pressure. "If you don't stop..."

She responded with more pressure as she suckled him. His balls clenched in warning. His whole body tensed as the orgasm began. He groaned as he squirt his semen into her mouth.

"Oh, God. Riley." He tightened his grip on her head as his body went rigid with the release.

She let go and swallowed. It was the most beautiful, erotic, sexy thing he had ever seen.

He pulled her to her feet and kissed her hard, tasting his semen on her lips and tongue.

He pushed her backward until she was against the bed, then he laid her gently down.

He undressed her slowly, kissing every inch of skin as he exposed it. Riley squirmed beneath him, wanting him to touch her breasts, her vagina. The places that would drive her to the brink of insanity before allowing her the release she so desperately wanted. She thrust her hips upward.

"Oh, no. Slow and sexy for you."

She groaned.

"Pay backs are a bitch, aren't they?" He swirled his finger around her nipple, but didn't touch it. Riley thought she would go insane with want. He ran his hand over her thigh, down her calf, and back up the other side, but never went near her pussy. She was writhing on the bed, desperate for him.

"Shane, please."

"Tell me what you want Riley."

"I want you to lick me."

Shane licked her neck. "Here?"

She shivered. "No."

"Here?" He licked the underside of her breast.

"No! The nipple, Shane. Suck my nipple."

He did as she asked. "Like this?"

"Yes, dammit. Now the other one. And touch me with your hands, Shane. Now. Please."

Shane chuckled. He sucked one nipple while rolling the other between his thumb and forefinger. Riley was going wild beneath him. Her hands grabbing for the down comforter.

"Fuck me Shane. Hard and fast, please."

"Not yet, Riley. First this."

He licked down her stomach, and finally found her drenched pussy. He parted her labia and licked his way up to her clitoris. He flicked his tongue over the swollen nub and Riley screamed.

"Yes." She pushed his head downward. "More."

Shane sucked gently, then he worked his tongue in a rapid but steady pace that had Riley screaming his name. The spasms shook her as he continued to torture her clitoris and Riley rolled through two of the strongest orgasms she'd ever had. Tears welled in her eyes at the intensity of the pleasure.

Shane kissed her as he braced himself above her. "Help me in, baby. I have something else for you."

Riley reached between them and guided his rock-hard cock to her center. He slowly entered the moist hot depth of her pussy, pulled out then slid back in. "You are so hot."

Riley groaned. "Hard and fast Shane."

He pulled all the way out, barely touching her with the thick head of his cock. "If you say so."

Shane lifted her legs up in the air and impaled her, pumping hard and fast and deep. Her vagina tightened around his cock. "Oh yeah. That's it, Riley. Come for me."

She was panting as she met his strokes, allowing for even deeper penetration and then she shattered into a million pieces just as he began his own powerful release.

It wasn't until he collapsed beside her, pulling her with him so he could stay within her warmth that he realized he had forgotten to use a condom.

Again.

Chapter Eleven

Trevor Snow slammed his hands against the steering wheel. "Where the hell is that bitch?"

His cell phone vibrated in his shirt pocket.

"Fuck." Domino.

Trevor considered letting the call go to voice mail, but he knew deceiving Domino was a death sentence. "Sir?"

"What the fuck you doing, boy?"

"Waiting for the Blackstone girl, sir."

"The hell you are. She's gone dumb ass."

Trevor scanned the area again. His gaze stopping in the rearview mirror. Lights flashed behind him. He shuddered. Domino's men were watching him. Excuses would do him no good. He was toast.

"You still there, Trevor?"

"Yes, sir."

"You may want to encourage your sister to take a little trip until things cool down."

"She won't be a problem. I'll make sure of it." Trevor made some stupid choices in the last three years, but he wouldn't let his sister get caught in the middle of this war. He still had some conscience.

"Good to know. Find the girl. Two days. No excuses."

Trevor closed his phone, jammed it into the miniature compartment in the dash designed just for cell phones. He leaned back against the headrest.

Trevor didn't know how to get out of the tangled web his life had become. He really was a fly, caught in the silken web of the meanest SOB on the planet. One wrong move and Trevor would be dead. A horn blared behind him, snapping him out of his pity party.

His tail sped past, the passenger flipping him off.

"Yeah, fuck you too."

Trevor jammed the car into drive and pulled out onto the rain slicked road. The weather had been shit for days. Too warm for snow, but still colder than a well digger's ass. He hated the rain. At least when it snowed, he could ski and ride and take his snowmobile out into the wilderness.

Getting away sounded really good to him right now. But there was no running from Domino. Or was there?

Maybe his sister was the key after all. Maybe she and her new boyfriend could help him. Blackstone had connections. Trevor's stomach flipped as he considered the risk involved in turning on Domino. He could lose everything he spent the last three years acquiring: A fat house with a lake view, a trick BMW, and all the toys he loved to play with. But staying in the game was a risk too, to him and his family. They'd never been close, but Trevor felt so alone lately. The string of hotties The Basement provided for his enjoyment was getting old.

Maybe he was finally growing up.

Trevor drove through town, checking his mirrors, watching for the tail. When he felt safe, he drove back to the Blackstone house. Shane's car was in the drive, so Trevor continued down the street. He pulled over at the next block and grabbed his phone. He scrolled down to his sister's name.

Riley slipped out from under Shane's embrace, padded barefoot and naked into the bathroom. As she cleaned up, she ran through the chain of events that played out at Shane's house. His betrayal still stung, but she couldn't ignore the horror Katie witnessed. And what if Trevor played a role?

Donning her robe, she quietly closed the bedroom door and headed for the kitchen. As the coffee brewed, Riley stood at the window, watching the sun dance in and out of the riot of clouds looming over the mountain tops. She yawned, tired from the late night and lack of good sleep. She wondered if she made the right decision in forgiving Shane for his betrayal. She understood his motives and believed his feelings for her were genuine. And for those reasons, she could get past the deception. She hoped.

Riley's sham of a marriage to Robert taught her that she hadn't loved him and he hadn't loved her. They were convenient partner's playing house. Nothing more. Now, with perspective, it was so damned clear to her, but back then, she'd have sworn on a stack of bibles that she'd been in love.

What she felt for Shane went so much deeper than anything she had ever felt for Robert and she barely knew Shane. A dichotomy for sure. On the one hand, she should be furious with Shane for invading her privacy, for using her to get to her brother. On the other, she wanted to help him. Even if it meant ruining her brother's life.

Riley really didn't believe that Trevor was directly involved. Clearly, he knew something or he wouldn't be trying to keep her away from Shane. But why?

An inkling of a plan began to form in her mind. If she could get Trevor to talk to Shane...

The coffee sputtered and spit and Riley turned nearly jumping out of her skin at the unexpected sight of Shane leaning against the counter wearing boxer briefs and a smile. She'd been so wrapped up in her thoughts she hadn't heard him come in.

"Penny for your thoughts?"

Riley smiled, "That is so cliché. My thoughts are worth way more than a lousy penny." She went to him and kissed him softly on his stubble ridden cheek.

He wrapped his arm around her waist and pulled her against his body. "Probably, but as you can see, I don't have my wallet."

"Really?" she shimmied against his hardening penis. "Then what's that?"

Shane dropped his hands to her butt, cupping each cheek as he fitted her quivering pussy against his length.

Riley rotated her hips but she pushed on his shoulders. "I need coffee buddy, so move out of my way and put that thought on hold."

"Bossy woman," Shane said as he released her with a slap on the ass.

Riley dragged two oversized coffee mugs from the cabinet, filled each one with the dark aromatic brew, then turned to Shane. "We need to talk."

"Uh oh. That sounds as ominous as the clouds out there." But Shane went to the table and pulled out a chair.

"Would you mind getting dressed first? I can't think when you're half naked.

Shane grinned. "I have a feeling I'd rather have you not thinking right now."

"I'm serious Shane. Get dressed." Riley plopped down on the chair Shane had pulled out and pushed his coffee across table.

He watched, his expression sobering. "Be right back."

Riley continued her watching the clouds move across the sky and sipped at her coffee.

Shane returned quickly and sat down.

Shane expected Riley to give him the heave ho. Once again, she surprised him. She had a plan to get Trevor to talk.

After hashing out the details, he coaxed her back into the bedroom and made slow, sweet love to her. He hadn't thought he could feel so deeply but with Riley it was easy and it scared the hell out of him.

They showered together and while Riley dressed, Shane headed into the living room and called Nick.

"Shane?" Nick sounded agitated.

"Everything okay there?"

"Trevor's been parked down the street. Mostly sleeping. I can't imagine him as a killer, Shane. The guy lacks a certain...I don't know...level of intelligence?"

"Maybe. But he knows something and Riley has hatched a plan to get him to talk." Shane filled Nick in on the details. "Call me when everything is in place."

"Will do."

"By the way, how's Beth?" Shane couldn't resist.

"Still asleep on the couch."

Shane laughed as Nick dropped a couple of not so nice words before he disconnected the call.

Trevor jolted at the sound of the siren, bashing his knee on the steering wheel. "What the fuck?"

He shook his head from side to side, wondering at the noise blaring through his tired brain. Then he looked out the window at Shane's house and saw the smoke.

He nearly fell out of the car door when he opened it, only righting himself by grabbing hold of the chicken bar in the roof. He slowly stretched first one leg, then the other until he was confident his legs would carry him.

He stood, testing his legs, eyes focused on the house down the road. Riley. He had to help her. He wouldn't let his sister die. He ran.

The sirens grew louder, piercing his eardrums as he reached the front yard. He jumped over a snow bank and landed with wheezing lungs on the porch just as the front door opened.

Beth and the guy who'd been hanging out at Shane's poured out the door, coughing and sputtering as a cloud of smoke followed them outside.

"Where's Riley?" Trevor sucked in a lungful of the toxic air.

"Not here," Beth hissed, moving quickly from the porch and down the walk where she finally sank to the ground, trying to catch her breath.

Trevor followed. He needed to know where Riley was. If she died, he would never forgive himself.

"Where is she." He pulled Beth from the ground and shook her. "She was here earlier, wasn't she?"

"No, Trevor. She's at home." Beth pushed him away.

A cell phone rang and Trevor watched as the man who'd fallen from the house with Beth pulled her close to his side.

"Shane. Yeah. It's just smoke." Nick coughed.

Trevor grabbed the phone from him. "Where's my sister?" He spat into the phone.

"Put Nick back on, Trevor." Shane's voice deadly.

Nick reached out, wrapped his seriously large hand around Trevor's neck and took the phone. "Don't fuck with me, asshole."

Trevor didn't move. He couldn't. The grip on his neck lethal. Obviously, this guy is one of Shane's G-man friends. Trevor put his hands up in an 'Okay, I give up' gesture.

Nick squeezed just hard enough to cause Trevor to go weak in the knees. He ginned as Trevor went down, then released him and went back to Shane. "You on the way yet?"

"Be there in ten."

Nick pushed the end button and shoved his phone into his jeans pocket. He wrapped an arm around Beth, pulling her closer. "You okay?" They fled the house in jeans and shirts. Neither had shoes or a jacket and though Nick's adrenaline kept his body temperature up, Beth shivered.

"Uh huh. Cold though."

"I know. We should be able to get inside soon. You wanna wait in the car?" He pulled his keys from his pocket.

Beth coughed and nodded.

Chapter Twelve

S hane sped through town. "That son of a bitch thought Katie was in the house."

Riley grabbed the "Oh Shit" bar next to her head as Shane rounded a corner at a dangerously high speed. She remained quiet though, because Shane had shifted from the fun lover to an intense DEA Agent in the blink of an eye. Riley feared for her brother's life. The Shane beside her scared the curl right out of her hair.

Relieved when they rounded the bend to Shane's house, Riley finally breathed.

Shane slammed on the breaks, sending Riley forward. His arm dashed out to protect her as they came to a stop a couple houses away from Shane's.

"Sorry," he bit out, throwing the car door open and sprinting away.

"No problem." She said to no one. She climbed from the car and ran after Shane. She only hoped he didn't kill Trevor before she got there.

She watched in horror as Shane lifted Trevor more than a foot off the ground with one hand. But then Nick and Beth were there.

"Put him down, Shane." Nick said.

"I didn't do this. I swear." Trevor's voice shook. "I thought my sister was in there. I wouldn't hurt her."

Shane looked past Trevor to Riley.

"Is she okay?" Trevor tried to look around but Shane held him firm.

Riley nodded at him and he dropped Trevor, literally. Her brother grunted as he hit the ground.

"I'm right here Trevor." Riley stepped into his line of sight. "What are you doing here?"

Trevor didn't answer, instead he looked around at the commotion.

"She asked you a question, dickhead." Shane lunged forward and Trevor scrambled to his feet.

"I can't talk out here," Trevor's words were just above a whisper.

Shane and Nick exchanged glances suspicion clear in both of their expressions.

"Should we bust him up and make it look good?" Nick asked.

"This shithead? It'll be my pleasure."

Trevor backed away, but the look on his face was agonized consent.

"Shane?"

Shane reached for her hand and gently squeezed it. Before Riley could react, Beth was dragging her away to the warmth and safety of Nick's car.

When the door was closed, Beth turned to her. "They won't really hurt him, Riley. They just have to make it look good."

"I don't understand?"

"Trevor was outside all night. Nick had someone watching him, just in case. He never left his car. Someone jumped the fence and threw something through the back window. Nick made sure the fire went out but to make it look good, he set his own fire to cause a huge amount of smoke."

Riley's mind was reeling trying to follow Beth's story. But at least Trevor was in the clear. That much she understood.

Riley wavered between anger, sadness and fear.

Riley knew her brother needed help. He needed help a long time ago. But their parents were in denial. They didn't know his attitudinal problems went deeper than the older-brother-jealous-of-his-little-sister syndrome. He demonstrated manic, narcissistic, behavior. Nothing Riley could do would ever really help him because he carried so much resentment toward her that he would almost go in the opposite direction just to spite her.

"They're dragging Trevor to a sheriff's department vehicle." Beth offered in a quiet voice. She took Riley's hand in hers. "This is good, Riley. They're protecting him."

"From what?" Riley looked up, made eye contact with her brother. He gave her a lopsided shrug. She looked down at Beth's hand, holding hers.

Her friend sighed. "From himself, partly, but especially from Domino."

Riley shivered. "Is that possible?"

"You're safe now, you little prick." Shane slammed the door to the only interrogation room at the El Dorado County Sheriff's Department. "Start talking."

Nick leaned against the battleship gray wall. Riley and Beth watched through the one-way glass. Riley insisted she would be able to read Trevor better than anyone. Shane figured he'd give her a shot.

Trevor stared at the glass. Did he know Riley was behind it?

Shane waited.

Nick paced.

Shane leaned on the back legs of his chair. Calm. Pissed. Patient. Angry.

Finally, Trevor looked at him. "I need protection. They'll kill me."

"I'm sure the County will put you up for a while."

"No." Trevor looked at the one-way glass, pleading. "He'll still get me. You and Nick," Trevor nodded in Nick's direction, but his gaze darted back to Shane. "Only the two of you."

"Did you kill my parents?"

"No."

"Do you know who did."

Nick moved closer to the table, but still had his back to the wall.

Trevor tapped his foot in a staccato beat. Seconds ticked past, turning to minutes.

Shane waited.

Nick paced, again.

The tapping stopped. "Protection. You and Nick." Trevor resumed his tapping.

Nick dragged a chair from the corner, turned it around and straddled it, resting his arms on the chair back. "Look, you little fuck. You really aren't in the position to bargain." Nick raised his hands, palms up and moved them up and down offering one or the other "Jail or talk. Which is it?"

Trevor stopped the staccato, crossed his arms over his chest and shut down.

Riley stared at the three men in the next room. She'd never seen Trevor so afraid. "He definitely knows who killed Shane's parents." Riley leaned against the windows edge. "He may have even played a part in their murder."

"Oh, Riley." Beth reached out and grasped Riley's hand. "I'm so sorry."

Riley couldn't imagine what kind of trouble Trevor had gotten himself into to get mixed up in murder. He had always been a bit of a trouble maker as a child. As he grew up, the antics worsened, but their parents thought it was all normal teenage angst.

Riley disagreed. His narcissism had been apparent. His I'm-the-center-of-the-universe attitude was ignored until he finally got arrested. After court fees, fines, and huge arguments, Trevor ran away, at sixteen.

Riley's mother cried for days, her father buried himself in his job, and Riley had been ignored. Her relationship with Trevor filled with resentment, animosity and a level of indifference, but he was her brother and she didn't want to see him harmed. Or in jail, if the truth be told.

Riley started for the door.

"Where are you going?" Beth asked, as she followed Riley.

"To talk to Trevor." She reached for the doorknob. "If he doesn't want to talk to Shane, he can talk to me. Maybe he'll take my advice for once."

"Yeah, and Lake Tahoe will freeze over." Beth reached out and stopped Riley from opening the door. "Come on, Riley. You know Trevor won't listen to you. You might only make it worse." Beth had known Trevor for a long time, and witnessed first-hand the horrible ways in which he treated Riley.

"Maybe, but I have to try."

Riley convinced the Deputy standing outside the interrogation room's door to open it for her. Seconds ticked past as she planned her strategy.

When the door opened, Shane appeared and pushed her back into the hallway. "What's up?" The door wasn't closed completely so Shane whispered.

"If I get him to talk, will you consider protecting him?" Riley knew her question would be hard for Shane. If Trevor was involved in any way in the death of his parents, he wouldn't help Trevor. He'd want to kill him.

Shane closed his eyes, clearly, fighting to control his emotions. The door snapped shut and he took her hand, leading her down the hallway.

He found an empty office and pulled her inside, closing the door behind them. He took a deep breath and looked at her. The storm brewing in his eyes made Riley's heart hurt.

"Shane, I know this is hard for you," She reached out, wanting to touch him, then pulled back. "If my brother was involved, I will help you put him away, but for now, we have to let him believe we're on his side."

Shane's eyes widened. "Did you just say you would help put him away?"

"Well, yes. If he's guilty, he deserves to go to jail." Riley shoved down the urge to cry. "He's my brother, but he's spent his whole life getting away with things. I don't want to see him in jail, but it's better than dead. And someday he has to pay for his behavior. If he killed your parents," Riley swiped at the tear sliding down her cheek, "then he needs to be punished."

Shane wrapped her in his embrace. "I'm so sorry, Riley."

She let go of her tightly held self-control and let the tears claim her. She should be angry, but instead she felt regret. She didn't want to believe he was capable of murder.

Shane held her for several minutes. Once she was composed, she pulled away. "I need your promise, Shane."

He kissed her with such tenderness that her heart threatened to burst through her ribs. She was amazed at the depth of her feelings for this rough and tumble warrior. But it was the gentleness in him that truly stole her heart.

"I promise. I will protect him as far as possible, depending on his answers."

"Okay. Let me talk to him. Alone."

"No."

"Shane, please. Let me try."

The struggle danced in his eyes. Riley knew the moment he relented. "Stay on the opposite side of the table from him."

"I will."

Shane led Riley back to Trevor. They reached the interrogation room and Shane opened the metal door.

Riley's stomach did a couple of back flips.

Shane turned to her. "Be careful."

She reached up laid her palm against his cheek. "I'll be fine."

Nick moved toward the door. "Riley thinks she can get him to talk," Shane whispered. "I agreed to protection, you and I. If it makes sense."

Nick only nodded as he stepped aside to let them pass.

Shane escorted Riley inside, never taking his eyes off of Trevor.

Riley settled into the chair, careful to keep her head lowered so she could compose herself before facing her brother.

"We'll be right outside if you need us." Shane squeezed her shoulders.

"Remember when we were kids and Mom and Dad took us to the Redwood Forest?" Riley didn't wait for a reaction. She stared at her hands, which lay flat on the table. "We'd been hiking through the woods for hours, trying to find the path that took us to the beach. Dad said he'd hiked the route many times in his youth, but we were lost and you knew it." Riley took a drink of water from the cup Nick had brought her before he and Shane closed the door. "Dad didn't want to listen to your ideas. He was like that a lot with you. He never listened to your side. Always jumped to conclusions. I always hated that. I wanted to help you, but when I tried, you'd yell at me. Call me names. You actually made me doubt myself on so many levels. I don't think you knew how much I looked up to you. How much I wanted you to like me.

Riley looked up then.

Trevor stared at her, sadness swimming in his eyes.

"When I was a little girl, I thought it was so cool having a big brother to protect me, but something changed and you became so mean. For years, I thought I was a fat, ugly pig, because you had called me one so many times. I believed you. I would've believed anything you said once. But even after all of that I miss my big brother, Trev. I want him back." Riley reached across the table and took his hand in hers, her gaze never leaving his.

"Is there any chance that my brother is in there somewhere? Any chance that you'll come back to me?"

Trevor pulled his hand away. Warring emotions played across his face. Riley waited to see if Trevor would revert back to his usual, I'm the victim, feel sorry for me ways.

He shook his head, cleared his throat. "I'm sorry, Riley." And the dam burst. Tears dropped down his cheeks.

"It all started when I moved here." He swiped at the last of the tears. "I went to work in the restaurant, waiting tables. After work we'd party at The Basement. One night, one of the guys offered me a line of cocaine. I felt like a fucking stud when I did coke." He stopped talking for a second, thinking back. Shadows clouded his eyes. "Domino offered me the chance to experience the best sex ever. Who could say no the that? The coke took away any inhibitions so I said hell yeah. He made me a drink, laced with some kind of super sex drug. I had a hard on for days and the best freaking sex ever. Women kept coming in and out...sorry. I probably don't need to go into detail."

Riley nodded. She didn't want to hear about any of this, but she had to know the truth. "Go on."

"I started doing coke every day, and every night I would pay for the sex Domino had made sure I would crave. He sucked you in with the drugs and the girls. Pretty soon I couldn't pay my bills so he made me an offer. I sold my fucking soul to the devil."

Trevor started to get up, but Riley reached across the table to stop him. "What did he make you do, Trev?"

"One of those first nights when all the women were coming and going, he videotaped the sex. The girl was underage. Four-fucking-teen. He told me if I didn't follow his orders, he would show the video to the girls' parents and I'd go to jail for statutory rape." Trevor dropped his head in his hands.

Minutes ticked past as Riley waited for Trevor to continue. Finally, he looked up. His expression, beaten, ashamed, disgusted. "I started selling drugs for him, then moved up to pimping out the girls. At first, I loved the money. Bought my house, the coolest toys. Had my pick of women every day. But every day I dropped deeper into hell. I beat up one of the girls when she wouldn't do what I wanted her to. Domino had some big buff body builder that worked for him and for Blackstone beat the crap out of me. Blackstone saw it happen and tried to help me. Then one day the dude was working out at the gym and was bragging about all the sex he was having with young girls and Blackstone overheard him. A few weeks later I heard Domino talking about Blackstone and how he was sticking his nose in where it didn't belong. I don't know what he learned and what he had on Domino, but one night I was sent to the Blackstone house. I was only supposed to stake it out to see if the guy from the gym was there."

Riley gasped. She turned around and looked at the glass behind her. "Oh, God. Is that the night the Blackstones were killed?" She turned back to Trevor. His gaze fixed on the one-way glass behind Riley, he answered. "Yes. But when I saw what was happening, I tried to stop it, Riley. I swear."

Riley knew Shane must be in his own living hell right now and she wanted so badly to go to him and comfort him. But now she needed to be here for Trevor. He looked so lost and so dejected.

Her heart broke for the young boy she remembered. The one lost and alone and reaching out to her now. So much had happened. But her brother needed her help now. She wouldn't let him down. And maybe when this was all over, they could rebuild the bond that had held them so close for the first ten years of her life.

Chapter Thirteen

Shane stared through the one-way glass. Riley had Trevor singing like the proverbial canary.

Shane was proud of her. She stayed composed, focused and without emotion as he told his story.

When Trevor stopped talking, Shane began to pace. His mind raced.

"You're in deep, aren't you?" Nick's question didn't surprise Shane. His friend knew him better than anyone ever would, except maybe Riley.

"She had me at hello."

Nick laughed. "Not true. You were fascinated at hello."

"Yeah."

Nick turned away. "But something changed today."

"Yeah." Something had changed today. Big time. He'd lost his heart to Riley. Completely. He knew it yesterday and even then, he tried to fight it. It scared the shit out of him.

"So, what's the plan." Nick knew when to back off. That was the thing about their friendship.

"Not sure yet, but we need to get Riley out of there and get Trevor to a safe house."

"But he expects us to protect him. We can't do that if he's in a safe house."

Shane smiled. "But we will be protecting him, indirectly." Shane punched a number into his phone. "Jake, it's Shane. I have a job for you."

Nick chuckled. "You are a devious son-of-a-bitch."

Shane nodded, turned away from Nick and filled Jake in on the events of the last few hours. He paced as he spoke with Jake. Shane knew Riley would fight him when he explained his reasons for wanting her to go with Trevor, but he had to keep her safe too.

He disconnected the call. "Jake won't be ready for us for a couple of hours. As you heard, Riley and Beth will go with Trevor. Any ideas on how we convince them to go?"

"Convince who to go where?" Riley asked as she and Beth entered the room.

Riley's talk with Trevor left her exhausted; both emotionally and physically. She wanted to go home and crawl into bed, alone.

Beth waited in the hall outside of the interrogation room. She hugged Riley tightly as though sensing Riley was on the edge of a break down.

Riley slid into a chair, wincing as the thick metal back bit into her shoulders. Shane knelt in front of her, taking her hands in his.

"You did great in there." Shane said softly.

Riley looked up into the sexy green eyes she had come to adore. Something in his tender gaze shattered the last of her resolve. She leaned forward into his shoulder and cried. She cried for Shane and Katie and the loss of their parents. She cried for Trevor, who would probably end up in jail when all of this was over. She cried for her parents who would have to face the truth of their son's depravity. She cried for herself and the loss she felt even though she had lost her brother years ago.

When the tears slowed, Riley pulled away from Shane's embrace and stood. "I need to go home."

"I'll take her," Beth offered as Shane stepped away.

He knew Riley needed some space and some time to regroup. He would give her that, but only for a couple of hours, which of course he did not share with her or Beth. He and Nick would move them to Jake's, eventually.

He brushed a strand of hair away from her face and gently kissed her on the forehead. "I'll see you later, baby."

Riley only nodded as Beth led her from the room. Nick followed, he would drive them to Riley's house and keep an eye on them. When Riley was settled, he would explain the plan to Beth.

Shane watched Riley walk down the hall. He ached for her. Having to hear the truth about her brother's lifestyle left her tortured and filled with a heartache Shane could only imagine. He turned back to the one-way glass and watched as Trevor stared back.

He tried to feel something other than rage for the broken man staring at the glass. He couldn't even feel the slightest degree of pity, even though Trevor was Riley's flesh and blood. Not just because he had played a role in the death of Shane's parents, but because he had torn a hole in the heart of the woman Shane loved. Though the feelings of protectiveness that surged through his soul were new to him, Shane felt them deeply and took his role seriously. She had crept into his heart the second he kissed her and the more time they spent together, the tighter her hold became, until she had him completely. Heart and soul. He will kill anyone who hurt Riley and right now he wanted to kill Trevor on so many levels. His fists clenched at his sides and his jaw tightened as he watched the weak little man beyond the glass.

Shane thought that knowing who killed his parents would somehow ease the pain, the anger, the rage. It didn't. Now he had to catch the son-of-bitch and keep his sister and the woman he loved safe in the process.

Even when he took Domino down, Shane knew the scumbag would still have the power to get to any or all of them. He had to figure out how to protect them all from the criminal's far reaching hands.

Shane rolled his shoulders, unclenched his fists and left the room. He would need help to set his plan in motion, but first he needed to make the necessary arrangements to get Trevor and Riley to safety.

As soon as they were in the car, Riley called her parents. They planned to leave early tomorrow morning to come up for a visit. Riley had to stop them from coming, but she didn't want to talk to her mom right now. Thank God they didn't answer the phone. She left a message telling them something had come up, that she needed to help Beth with a personal family issue and she wouldn't be home this weekend after all. She finished the call with the usual "I love you both" and she'd check in later to reschedule the visit.

Mostly the truth. Something had come up. Her brother was a criminal, a depraved, abusive sex addict and a participant in the death of Shane's parents.

Riley didn't know how to process her feelings. The anger, shame and guilt ate at her like termites eating wood. She had fallen in love with Shane and she couldn't help but wonder if it would be best to walk away from him. How would he ever love her knowing her brother had been partly responsible for tearing apart his family.

Riley swiped a tear from her cheek as she leaned down to start the shower.

Leaving her clothes in a puddle on the bathroom floor, Riley checked the water temperature, stepped under the hot spray and let the sob she'd been holding back break free. Tears slid down her cheeks, mixing with the water and swirling down the drain. She made her decision without even realizing it. She would help Shane and then she would let him go.

When the water became too cold to stand, Riley wrapped a thick towel around her and crawled into bed. She hadn't planned to sleep. She only wanted to hold the pillow with the lingering scent of Shane and their earlier lovemaking.

She awoke with a start, confused by the darkness in the room. Voices penetrated her conscience and she reached for the light on the bedside lamp. The clock display said two-fifteen. Riley untangled her limbs from the bedding and grabbed the still damp towel from her bed and took it to the bathroom. She had to spray her hair with water to dampen it so that she could control the spiking curls and tame the bed head she'd awakened with. She brushed her teeth, dressed in comfortable jeans and a sweatshirt and headed in the direction of the voices.

She found Beth asleep on the couch, Shane and Nick at the dining room table, drinking coffee. Shane looked exhausted and guilt clutched at Riley's heart. He stood, a hesitant smile curving his lips.

"Hi," he said as he moved to pull her into his arms.

She let him hold her, but she didn't wrap her arms around him and when he tensed, Riley wanted to run from the room.

"I'm sorry, Shane." She offered as she pulled away from him.

"For what?" He reached for her hand, not willing to break the contact she fought to avoid.

"Everything. My brother. Your parents." She pulled her hand free and busied herself with getting coffee.

Shane came up behind her, took the cup away and wrapped his arms around her. His lips grazed her neck as he whispered in her ear. "Don't do this Riley. It's not your fault."

Riley relaxed into him, wanting desperately to believe he would be able to forgive her. That they would be okay when this was over. She didn't want to lose him, what they shared. Not just the passion but the love. She could feel his heart, but she couldn't stand the knowledge that he might hold her even a little bit responsible for her brother's actions. Even though she knew it was ridiculous, she couldn't help but think his love for her would be affected.

Riley turned in his arms, allowed him to kiss her. The tenderness in his touch made her want to cry all over again.

"We need to talk," Shane said as he let go and picked up her coffee cup. "Sit down. I'll fix your coffee."

Riley went to the table, slipping into the chair across from Nick. His expression remained neutral, verging on bored.

Shane handed her the mug and sat down beside her, reaching across the table for his own coffee.

"We're picking Trevor up soon, then taking you, Beth and Trevor to a friends."

Riley nodded. She knew Shane would stash her away somewhere. She expected it. He and Nick would go in with guns blazing to take down Domino.

It would be pointless to argue, so Riley listened as Shane outlined the plan. When he finished, she went to her room to pack a bag with the items she would need for a couple of days. Her heart broke a tiny piece at a time with every step she took because she was so afraid. How would she survive losing Shane?

Shane tried to keep his emotions in check. Hell, he trained for years to be an unemotional warrior, but where Riley was concerned, he was lost in an abyss.

Trevor sat quietly in the back as they drove down the bumpy road leading to the Angora Lakes Recreation Area. The drove along a ridge on the west side of Fallen Leaf Lake; the area remote with only one road in.

Jake Brocade, an ex-SEAL and longtime friend of Shane's ran a guide service for extreme hiking and camping trips into the Desolation Wilderness.

Shane glanced in the mirror again at Riley. She gnawed at her lower lip her forehead creased with worry. Shane knew she was pulling away from him. He felt it deep down and there was nothing he could do to stop it. At least not yet. The strength and determination in her need to pull away made him want her even more than he already did. At some level she thought he needed her to pull away. She believed he held her responsible for his parents' death because of her brothers association with Domino. But she couldn't be more wrong. He didn't blame her. At all.

Shane ached with the need to tell her how much he loved her. But he knew she wouldn't believe him. Not yet. Not until this was over.

He forced his attention back to the road just in time for a curve. He slowed, then steadied the Land Rover. The blacktop turned to hard packed dirt and rock. They jostled over the terrain and into a parking area. Shane stopped in front of a gate and opened his door. Jake materialized in front of him.

"How the hell do you do that?" Shane asked, climbing from the car.

"If I told you..."

"Yeah. I know. You'd have to kill me." Shane grasped Jake's hand to shake, then pulled him into a bear hug.

The men clapped each other on the back and parted.

"What kind of pond scum have you brought me?"

Rustling leaves snapped Shane's attention to the forest behind Jake. A powerful yellow lab came charging at them through the dense Manzanita. Jake turned, raised his hand in the air. The dog came to a screeching halt.

"Chance, I told you to stay." The dog barked at Jake, who shook in head. "The dog has a mind of his own." Jake dropped his hand and

Chance closed the distance and sat at his master's side. "Back to the pond scum."

Shane glanced at the car. Riley opened the door and was climbing out, but Trevor stayed put, staring straight ahead, his expression stoic and resigned.

"Trevor Snow. A bouncer at The Basement and a lackey for Domino."

Jake's brows rose over the rims of his shades. "Who's the hot redhead?" He grinned at Shane's scowl.

"Riley Snow." Riley stopped beside Shane who put his arm out and pulled her to his side.

Jake laughed.

Chance barked.

Shane winced at the tug of jealousy pulling at his gut like a bird yanking a worm from the ground. Jake was crazy in love with a black-haired beauty named Jenna. They'd been through hell and back and come out the other side stronger than Shane thought two people could be together.

Riley looked from Shane to Jake. "What's funny?"

Chance barked again. Riley reached out and rubbed the dogs' ears. He remained seated, which impressed the hell out of Shane. He'd always wanted a dog, but his lifestyle wasn't conducive to pet ownership. Someday, he would settle down and get a dog. Maybe sometime soon.

The very notion terrified him. He'd never been one to stay in one place for very long. Even as a kid, he needed adventure: the more the adrenalin rush, the better he liked it.

He skied out of bounds at all the local resorts. Climbed mountains in the snow and skied down over rocks and trees. He'd ridden dirt bikes and jet skis and anything else he could find that went fast and gave him that rush.

But as he watched Riley, a strange constriction in his chest had him thinking of houses and kids and dogs. He shook his head, trying to fight the thoughts flooding his mind. *Get a grip, Shane. You don't do forever.*

"His name is Chance. Mine is Jake." Jake took his glasses off. "Nice to meet you, Riley." He smiled and extended his hand.

Riley took his hand and Shane noticed how Jake held on longer than he needed to. He also noticed the appreciation in Jake's gaze.

Nick and Beth joined them and when introductions were over, Shane went to the SUV to get the bags from the back. Trevor finally climbed from the vehicle, an oversized backpack in his hand.

No one said a word as he stood off to the side, but Jake looked him over with annoyance, then turned back to Riley.

"I'm afraid my house is pretty small. You and Beth can have the loft." Jake's gaze slid to Trevor, who looked ashamed and filled with guilt. Jake clearly didn't feel sorry for him, "He can have the recliner." Jake turned away from the group and headed down the trail.

Shane fought to hold back his grin. Jake's loyalty only went so far. He'd protect Trevor, but he wouldn't like it and he wouldn't treat him well. Shane regretted that he had to leave Beth and Riley in the same county with Trevor, but he had no choice.

Riley hadn't spoken to her brother since the day before in the interrogation room. She hadn't even acknowledged him when they picked him up from the Sheriff's Department. Shane handed Beth's bag to Nick, which made his friend scowl. Shane smiled. Nick had the hots for Beth, but had yet to act on his desire.

Shane caught up with Riley. "You okay?"

"How long do we have to stay here, Shane?"

"I don't know. I'll do my best to wrap things up quickly, I promise." He squeezed her hand to reassure her, though he didn't feel very confident at the moment. He and Nick had tossed around several ideas, but so far, they didn't have a concrete plan.

Shane figured by the time they got back to town Nick would have something figured out.

Jake gave everyone the nickel tour of his cabin. It was small, but it had suited Jake well before he met Jenna. Now he lived in town with his wife and only stayed here to prepare for his guide trips.

Shane lingered in the loft while Riley set her purse on the desk beside Jake's computer. Everyone else went back downstairs.

"Come here." Shane pulled Riley into his arms. He hated the look in her eyes. The detachment. "Stop pulling away from me."

He kissed her then, deeply and with a hunger he only felt with her. She was slow to respond but when she did, Shane felt her sorrow, her fear. He ran his hands over her back, soothing her tension but soon they landed on her bottom. He pulled her closer, pressing his erection into her stomach. She moaned with need and he responded. He pushed her backward until she was against the wall, then he ran his hands under her sweatshirt, found her taut nipples and tugged gently.

She managed to get her hands between their bodies and pushed at his chest, "Shane, we can't do this now." She whispered on a rush of air.

"Yes, we can."

He silenced her protests with a kiss and proceeded to unzip her jeans, pushing them down with one hand while he slid a finger into her wet folds, finding her clit hard and swollen.

She moaned into his mouth as her tongue tangled with his. She tilted her pelvis upward to increase the pressure of his hand. That was all the encouragement he needed. He released his erection from his jeans and slid into her while he continued to tease her clit with his finger and fuck her mouth with his tongue.

The mating was hard and fast, filled with hunger and need and when Riley came, he swallowed her scream and then allowed himself to come.

Once he had his breath back, he kissed her gently. "I love you," he whispered hugging her tightly.

He heard her startled whimper and pulled back as he pulled out of her. A single tear slid down her cheek. She swiped it away and righted her clothing, then she placed her hands on his cheeks, pulled him to her and kissed him tenderly.

Shane couldn't help but feel as if she was saying goodbye.

Chapter Fourteen

R iley went into the bathroom and cleaned up. She wiped the last tears from her eyes, tried to convince herself that she could live without touching Shane again. She thought when he first told her that her brother might be involved with the death of his parents' they could withstand whatever came their way, but the truth was, Riley couldn't handle it.

She couldn't handle always wondering if Shane blamed her, even the slightest bit. She knew at some level the idea of him blaming her made no sense at all. Still, she couldn't let it go.

She dug in her bag for her earbuds, needing to lose herself in something other than thoughts of Shane. She heard him say goodbye to Jake, heard the door close.

Pushing play, Riley listened to her favorite songs while rocking back and forth in the old chair. She looked up when Beth came into the room.

Riley took the earpieces out of her ears, turned off the music and waited for her friend to settle into the chair next to her.

"You okay?" Beth asked, a knowing look in her eyes.

"I will be."

"You know, he doesn't blame you. In fact, I'd bet the royalties from your first best seller that he's in love with you."

Riley smiled sadly. "He told me he loved me just a few minutes ago. But it doesn't change anything. I can't forgive what my brother did, who he is..."

"Knock it off, Riley. You're looking for an excuse to run away. Dare to live your truth! You found a man you can really love, one who appreciates you, respects you, and cherishes you. I can see it in his eyes. Every time he looks at you, it's with awe. Do you know how special that is? You really want to walk away?"

Riley thought her tears were all used up, but her eyes filled as she listened to Beth. The truth in her friend's words hurt, because Riley knew Beth was right. She was terrified at how much she'd grown to love Shane in such a short time and she didn't know if she could survive truly loving him, let alone losing him. If she pushed him away first, she thought she might have a chance of surviving without him.

Beth stood, looked around the room that used to be Jake's bedroom according to the rundown he'd given them earlier during the brief tour of his cabin. The room was large, the same size as the entire downstairs that consisted of a kitchen, dining area, living room and bathroom. The loft area had a bed, desk, two comfortable chairs, likely used for reading or just relaxing. The space screamed rugged and very male. Practical.

Beth went to the window and stared outside. "I remember when you told me Robert proposed. You were matter-of-fact, but not the least bit excited. I wondered why you would marry someone who didn't adore you, who you didn't adore. But for a while you were happy and I was jealous." Beth turned back to Riley. "You had found the happily-ever-after and I still hadn't managed to stay in a relationship for more than six months. I envied you so much."

Riley waited, sensing her friend had more to say.

"Then you called and told me about Robert's affair and part of me was happy because you were going to be single again and we would be able to hang out more. I wouldn't have to be jealous anymore."

Shocked at Beth's admissions, she closed the space between them.

Beth reached for Riley's hand. "I'm so sorry for feeling like that. I would never wish you pain or unhappiness, but I felt relieved."

Riley hugged her friend, grinning inwardly at the irony. "I always hated that you got the good-looking guys when we were growing up. I was always jealous of you. I had no idea you ever felt that way."

"And now you have a man truly deserving of your love. One who will love you back, deeply and honestly and you're going to run away?"

"I don't know if I'm strong enough to love Shane." And that was the truth of it.

Beth groaned, placed her hands on each of Riley's cheeks and looked into her eyes. "Of course, you are. Get past the fear. Because if you push him too far away, you will regret it."

Before Riley could respond, she heard Jake shout at Trevor to stop. Beth and Riley raced downstairs in time to see Jake pin Trevor against the opened front door.

"You are to stay inside unless I say otherwise." The order carried a deadly threat that had the hairs on Riley's arms standing up. "The only reason you're still alive is because of your sister, otherwise Shane would have ripped you in half and fed you to the bears you, sorry son-of-bitch. So, don't fuck with me."

The look on Trevor's face wavered between rage and fear. He glowered at Riley as though she was to blame. Just like when they were kids, he always blamed her. When Jake released his hold, Trevor went to the couch and dropped down silently.

Riley shot out the door and ran to the edge of a small lake twenty feet from cabin. Chance followed her, sitting beside her as she sank to her knees in the sand. She reached out to the dog, rubbing his ears. The dog licked her, making her smile.

"He's good therapy." Jake's voice was soft, laced with concern. "Sorry for that scene back there. This must be hard for you."

"You have no idea."

"I think I do." Jake sat down on the other side of Chance, who decided to lay down and roll onto his back for a belly rub. "My wife almost died at the hands of her father, the same man who raped her mother. They both managed to survive the guilt, the shame and the pain. So, can you. And if you let Shane help you -- there's nothing you won't be able to handle."

Riley didn't respond for a long time. "How long have you known Shane?" Riley looked at Jake for the first time.

"Since high school. We played football together, went into the Navy together."

"So that would be pretty well then?"

Jake laughed, the sound comforting. "You could say that. Yes."

"Do you think he'll blame me for being the sister of the person who helped to kill his parents?"

Jake's eyes darkened in color, simmering with intensity Riley had seen in Shane's eyes several times. "No. Never."

Riley looked out at the pristine lake, rippling in the light wind. She imagined this area would be a place she would find great comfort in under normal circumstances. Peaceful. Beautiful. Serene. Secluded.

Shane's face floated before her mind's eye. Passion filled. Her heart constricted. Maybe she could dare to take a chance. Maybe she would dare to trust.

Jake's cell chirped, and Riley thought the ring tone too gentle for the warrior beside her.

"Talk to me," he said quietly. He listened for a time his expression fixed. Unchanging. "Okay, I'll let them know. Good luck."

Riley watched the water ripple. Chance dragged himself up from his lazy nap and waited as Jake stood. He held out his hand.

Riley grabbed hold and allowed herself to be pulled up. "Was that Shane?"

"Yes."

Riley walked beside Jake without asking questions. His clipped response told her to move it and he would tell everyone at the same time. She understood why Shane called Jake. The man exuded strength and competence. Riley felt secure with him. She trusted him.

Trevor looked up when they came into the room.

"Where's Beth?" Jake asked as he closed and latched the door.

Trevor simply shifted his gaze upward.

No one called to her, but she came down the stairs as though she'd been summoned.

Jake outlined the plan Shane had shared with him, not offering any additional information or comments. Riley suspected he knew more than what he told them, but didn't push it. Jake's history alone prevented him from sharing too much. He certainly wouldn't tell her where Shane and Nick were and what they were up to.

Chapter Fifteen

Shane disconnected the call to Jake. Riley and Beth were safe. Trevor remained silent and stoic. Still, Shane had a bad feeling in the pit of his stomach. Maybe the pounding music caused his discomfort, maybe the danger he and Nick might face with this crazy fishing expedition flipped his insides and jacked up the hair on the back of his neck.

The feeling increased as he and Nick descended into the dark and smoky depths of The Basement in an attempt to physically tie Domino to the explosion that took the lives of Shane's parents.

Shane had donned a blonde wig and mustache, garnering a jab from Nick that he looked akin to a WWF wrestler. Shane jabbed his friend at the insult but laughed. He did resemble an overrated-pretty-boy-tough guy.

Nick didn't need extreme. He added a pair of glasses and a wig that lengthened his hair and even Shane had trouble recognizing him. His shape-shifting talent always put Nick at the top of his class in any assignment.

They fought their way through the crowded dance floor to the bar. Each ordered a beer and headed for the back wall which allowed a view of the floor and the hallway that led to the offices where Domino spent most of his time.

"Check that out," Nick said, motioning with a slight nod toward the corner.

Shane watched as a long-legged blonde bounced up and down on her partner's' lap. Though part of Shane found the scene erotic, he also found it disturbing.

Shane scanned the room, noticed several other couples engaged in indecent public behavior. He couldn't help but respond. He had to force his thoughts away from sex to keep his dick from hardening further. The curse of being a man.

The door leading to the private offices, and probably sex rooms, opened. Two bulky goons stepped through, squinting as in an effort to adjust to the darkness of the club's interior.

"This is our chance," Nick said as he headed for the door.

When they reached the muscle-heads, Shane pulled two bullet shaped devices from his pants pocket and popped both men simultaneously. Shane grabbed the one on the right, Nick the one on the left. They managed to get them back behind the door before the thugs slumped to the ground unconscious.

"You sure these are the only goons back here?" Shane asked.

Nick began surveilling The Basement the day Shane dragged him to Tahoe. "I'm sure. We have ten minutes until Tweedle-Dee and Twee-dle-Dum wake up."

"I'll take the right side, then." Shane moved down the hall, opening doors without a sound.

Behind door number one, Shane saw a man with two women. One impaled on his dick, the other squatting on his face. Door number two held two men and one woman. Shane had never had a threesome, but watching the woman with a dick in her mouth and one in her pussy caused his own cock to harden. Truth be told, he had never thought much about a threesome. Pleasing one woman took a serious amount of effort and skill. But what kind of pleasure would a woman find in having two cocks, four hands and two sets of lips roaming over and in her body?

He shook off the thought and focused on the task at hand, continuing down the ever-shortening hallway.

He and Nick met at the last door, which opened into a large suite. The first room a sitting area with an office to the right and a large, very sadistic looking bedroom to the left. Nick took the office while Shane began his search of the bedroom.

Shane would have preferred the office but Nick was the computer whiz and they needed the files on Domino's hard drive. The bedroom had all the gadgets of a practicing Dominant or a sexually depraved freak; handcuffs, ropes, ceiling swing and other various devices, including a double-sided dildo. He wondered how far from the edge Domino took his little games.

He entered a plush bathroom with a shower head in the ceiling and a large sunken hot tub. After a careful search, he found nothing that would lead to the downfall of Domino, except a couple of cameras. He figured Nick had located videos or DVD's already.

On cue, Nick arrived. "Time's up."

They retreated, stepped over the hulks and blended back into the crowded bar. After ordering another beer, Shane and Nick chatted with a couple of women. Nick got so far into character that he danced a slow, but steamy dance with a large breasted blonde. The dance ended, Nick whispered something to the woman and turned away to join Shane.

They left The Basement and headed back to Shane's. Once there, Nick booted up his computer while Shane called to check on Riley.

Riley's cell phone went straight to voicemail, so Shane tried Jake's. Ditto.

"Nick, what's Beth's cell number?" Shane asked.

"Three one eight, five nine two nine. What's up?"

"Jake and Riley's cells are going straight to voicemail. I know Jake's works out there." Shane punched in the numbers Nick gave him. "Something's wrong," he said as Beth's voice mail came on.

Nick stood. "What kind of backup plan did Jake have arranged?"

Shane ran a hand through his hair. "The cabin at Echo Lake."

"Let's go." Nick pulled his laptop from the desk, dug around until he found the DC Adaptor and grabbed the two sticks containing Domino's computer files. "You drive."

Shane chose the Chevy Suburban over his Land Rover. His father had given his Mother the Beast when she wrecked her smaller Blazer a few years ago sliding on the ice. She had been bruised but uninjured. Still, his Dad wanted his Mom to be as safe as possible. He would have bought her a tank if he could have. Shane felt a little odd driving his mothers' car.

Nick got the laptop running and began the tedious search of Domino's files.

Shane tried to tamp down the fear churning his insides like a freaking ice cream maker. He punched Dr. Banks number into his phone. She answered on the third ring.

"Shane, is everything okay?"

"Sorry to call so late, but I need to know that Katie is alright."

"She's fine. I checked on her twenty minutes ago."

Shane relaxed, "Thanks."

"Shane, what's wrong?"

"Nick and I went to The Basement to look for evidence against Domino. We know he was involved in the explosion, that he ordered it." Shane felt his anger and pain break free. He forced it back into a safe place. "We stashed Beth and Riley at a friends house and now I can't reach any of them."

Dr. Banks lowered her voice. "I'll talk to security."

"I'd appreciate that, thanks." Shane wanted to ask to talk to Katie but stopped himself. He didn't want to upset her and he feared he wouldn't be able to keep the distress out of his voice.

"I hope everything's okay at your end. I'll check with you in the morning."

Shane disconnected the call as he started the climb up the summit. He drove as fast as the Suburban allowed, popping the vehicle into four-wheel drive at the Echo Road turn off. Two feet of snow covered the seldom driven road, making it almost impossible to drive with any amount of speed. At times the road narrowed to a single lane with trees on one side and a deep ravine on the other. In another month, it would be impassable.

"Gotcha!" Nick exclaimed as he punched at the computer keys.

"Proof?" Shane asked without taking his eyes from the road.

"Better." Nick snapped the laptop closed. "The fucker's death sentence."

Riley watched the neon green light stick move while Jake placed small devices in front of the windows in the small cabin. Beth held her hand in a vise grip. Somehow the pain eased the agony clutching at her heart.

Riley shivered.

"It'll be okay." Beth released her hand and pulled Riley into a sideways hug. "I'm so sorry about Trevor."

Riley needed to move. Sitting here, staring at the walls of the old forest service cabin, she felt so exposed. Both physically and emotionally. But there was nowhere to go. "What are those things?" she asked Jake.

"Motion sensors. I'm sure we're safe, but..." He put the light inside his flannel, drowning them in darkness. "I need to be sure." He knelt in front of Riley, touching her knee. "Shane will be here soon. He was supposed to call when they left The Basement. He knows we're here by now."

Riley hugged her knees tighter to her chest. She'd never been so scared.

She and Beth were in the kitchen, throwing together a dinner Riley hadn't cared to eat when the front window shattered, sending shards of glass across the room. She and Beth ducked behind the counter, avoiding the spray of glass. Chance barked as Jake ran outside. They heard shouting and gunshots but stayed silently on the kitchen floor, huddled together in fear.

Riley had thought she should call for Trevor, but fear coiled around her throat like a cobra, choking off her ability to speak.

Jake returned an eternity later. Riley and Beth peeked above the counter, standing when Jake nodded.

Riley screamed when she saw Trevor dead on the floor. Beth gagged, ran back to the kitchen. Riley barely heard her friend as she threw up. Nausea churned in her own stomach.

Jake wasted no time. He had closed Trevor's lifeless eyes and pulled her into his arms. He held her while she shook with grief, fear and horror. After a time, he set her apart from him with hands on her shoulders, and looked her in the eye. "I will get you back to Shane safely, but you have to listen to me without hesitation." Riley nodded and miraculously, here they were, in a small cabin in the middle of somewhere. She didn't remember how they had gotten here her shock had paralyzed her. But she was coming out of it.

She clamped her eyelids closed and pulled Shane's face into view. *Please hurry. I need you.* The words were her mantra. She repeated them over and over until she felt Jake tense.

He moved away from her and she shimmied closer to Beth. The silence in the small space was suffocating. Riley closed her eyes, but Trevor's lifeless expression filled the darkness. She shuddered, squeezing her eyes tighter, causing her tears to drown out the vision.

The sound of a powerful engine shattered the silence and Riley screamed. A second shriek filled the small space.

Beth.

She squeezed Riley as her body shook with fear.

And then Shane was there.

He pulled her to him. "It's okay, baby. It's me."

Riley needed Shane more than oxygen, but suddenly found herself getting angry at him. Her brother died in front of her. Shane was supposed to protect him.

She fought the anger, needing his comforting embrace more at the moment. She grabbed hold, wrapping her arms around his neck. Her body shook like the 1906 San Francisco earthquake.

Shane rubbed her back, whispering in her ear. She couldn't make out the words but the wracking shakes slowed as he held her. Tears pushed past her eyelids, sliding silently down her cheeks.

"I've got you. You're safe." Shane held on.

Somewhere in the distance she heard Nick soothing Beth as she cried. Then Beth's voice, quivering as she spoke. Little snippets snuck through to Riley's consciousness.

"Son-of-a-bitch." Shane spat as he pulled back, his breath no longer a whisper against her neck.

The light slipped through her eyelids causing Riley to open her eyes. An eerie green glow filled the room, illuminating Shane's face. Anger and anguish filled his features.

"I found a tracking device in his phone." Regret laced Jake's tone. "I should've checked."

"No. I should have checked." Shane grumbled.

"Fuck." Nick muttered.

Shane found Riley's hand. He pulled her against his side. "Jake, I need you to take Beth and Riley out of here. Take my car. Nick and I will get back to your place and take your Jeep back to town."

Riley ripped her hand from his, squaring off in front of him. "You promised to protect him."

Shane watched as Jake tucked the women into the Suburban. He had fucked this up. Again. He let down the person he loved the most. What the fuck was wrong with him. How had they overlooked the cell?

Nick came up beside him, "She's in shock, Shane. You'll work it out."

Shane shook his head. "She's right, though. It was my plan that got her brother killed." Why couldn't he do the right thing, be the right thing, just once?

Nick pulled Shane's arm, forcing his friend to spin around and look at him. "Don't go there, Shane. Domino had a bead on him already."

"Maybe." Darkness wrapped itself around Shane. He pulled out his penlight and headed toward Echo Ridge. He forced aside his hurt and shame. He and Nick needed to finish what they started. He would deal with the rest of it later.

The trails were slippery with snow and ice. Shane and Nick were prepared for such conditions and they made good time back to Jake's place.

Seeing Trevor laid out on the floor affected Shane worse than the terror and death he'd seen in the jungles of Columbia, because he knew how horrible it must have been for Riley and Beth. The warring pain in Riley's eyes, even as she tried to hold on to him for comfort, played in his mind's eye. He shook it off and got busy. Feeling sorry for himself would solve nothing. He'd take down Domino, then he would fight for Riley's forgiveness.

Shane called the Sheriff's Department, asking for his old friend Marc Attison. Someone in dispatch forwarded his call through to Marc's cell.

"Hey, Marc. It's Shane Blackstone. I have a mess out at Jake's place."

"I'm fine, Shane. How are you?"

Shane frowned as he stared at Trevor. "Not so good. Got a dead body, Marc."

"I'll get a team together and be there as soon as I can."

"Thanks."

Shane and Nick conducted their own version of crime scene investigating. Without disturbing evidence, they found the spent shell casing from the high caliber rifle that took off half of Trevor's head. They also found a cigarette butt and a trail of footprints.

The dumb fuck who took out Trevor would be easily found with the treasure map he'd left behind.

As he and Nick made their way back to the cabin, Shane fought to keep his thoughts from traveling too near Riley's expression. She witnessed Trevor's death, had seen the horror of his brain splintered and splashed around the room. How would she ever process that? Shane still had nightmares of the first time he watched a man die. Even though he was the enemy, Shane felt regret at having taken a life. He was sickened by the visceral destruction and by the stench when the body eliminated.

"Shane." Nick's voice broke through, dragging Shane back to the present. Nick knew where Shane had been. They'd all been there more than once.

"I'm okay." He turned toward Nick and waited as Marc approached.

Marc Attison was tall and lean. Shane had met him several years ago. He was a good cop, a better man, and more importantly, a good friend.

Shane gave Marc a half nelson hug. "How are you?"

"Better than you from the mess over there." Marc pointed at Trevor's body. "The coroner's on the way. What happened?"

"His name is Trevor Snow," Shane said without glancing in the direction of Trevor's body. "He worked for Joe Dominico. Long story short, he was involved in the death of my parents and implicated Domino. We stashed him with Jake while we did some...investigating. Domino found him and took him out."

Marc studied Shane for a long silent moment, then turned to Nick. "Nutshell, huh? Where's Jake?"

"He's taking Riley Snow and her friend Beth to San Francisco." Nick said, stepping up beside Shane and Marc. "He'll call you as soon as he's on the road to give you his statement. You can interview the women then too." Nick didn't wait for Marc's argument. "Footprints, cigarette butt and shell casings outside. Should be an easy solve for you."

Marc looked at Shane, then turned to Nick, "That right?"

"I have everything you need for a conviction on my laptop, but..."

"But we need to wait," Shane finished for Nick. "Domino has something else planned. We'll take him down when he makes his move."

Marc's eyebrows rose, "What could he possibly have planned that would supersede an arrest?"

Shane handed Marc his phone which displayed a picture from one of the files Nick found on Domino's computer. "Another murder."

"Holy shit." Marc looked from Shane to Nick, then back at the picture. "Holy shit."

"Exactly," Shane responded as he took the phone from Marc's shaking grasp.

Riley moved through packing another overnight bag in a fog of slow motion. Her heavy heart beat a steady thump against her chest, the ache drilling deeper as the vision of Trevor's lifeless eyes flashed in her memory. She squeezed her eyes closed, trying in vain to stop the scene from repeating itself. Tears leaked down her cheeks and she dropped to the floor, letting the floodgates open. A sob tore from her throat.

Riley felt Beth's arms go around her, heard her friend's' words of comfort but still she cried. She cried for the loss of her brother, even though they weren't close, they were family and once upon a time he had been her friend, her protector. A memory reel played in her mind's eye of she and Trevor as kids: running up and down the streams in the woods behind their house catching fish with their bare hands, hiking ten miles through the woods to go to a movie, trick-or-treating in the pitch black and scaring the others kids.

She cried for the loss of Shane. She trusted him to protect them and he failed. She thought him her soul mate. He touched her on so many levels. She felt whole with him. But he let her down, just like everyone else she ever loved. Except Beth. She held on to her friend as though she were a life preserver and Riley was adrift in a turbulent ocean.

When the tears were spent, Beth helped Riley into the bathroom where she splashed cold water on her face.

"Did you get all your stuff?" Beth asked as she opened the medicine cabinet.

Riley shook her head. Beth didn't look at her with pity, if she had, Riley would have lost it all over again. Instead, Riley felt stronger. She knew Beth must be freaked out too. She saw the horror too and yet she kept her fear and pain to herself so she could help Riley. But Beth's eyes were red and swollen, her complexion ashen.

Riley bent down, opened a drawer and pulled out a toiletry bag stocked with travel sized hair products. Beth added her friends make-up and led her from the room.

Riley picked up her overnight bag, looking with longing and loss at her bed, still mussed from the last bout of lovemaking. She fought to keep it together.

"I need my laptop."

Beth nodded taking the overnight bag from her as Riley went upstairs to her office. She packed her laptop and the latest stack of letters she needed to review for her next column.

She and Beth met Jake in the driveway. He took her bags and put them in the back of Shane's suburban. Riley climbed in the back seat with her laptop, hoping to distract her thoughts during the drive.

Jake took the long way through Reno to avoid driving back through the city limits of Tahoe. Riley didn't mind though, the thought of going home to San Francisco sharpened the pain still searing her heart.

She left San Francisco after her divorce, and never looked back. Now, as the darkness of the night shrouded her view of the mountains, she reflected on her childhood. Somehow Beth managed to sleep. Riley wished sleep would take her away right now. She wanted to hide in her dreams and pretend none of this had happened. But she couldn't. She would face her parents in a few short of hours.

Her heart tightened in her chest at the thought of her mother. How could she face her? How would she explain Trevor's death?

Chapter Sixteen

S hane left another message for Riley. The third. Her phone didn't even ring this time but went straight to voicemail. "She'll call when she's ready." Nick didn't look up from the blueprints he was studying. "She's still in shock, Shane."

"Yeah." Shane dropped onto the couch beside his friend. "Did you find a way into Domino's yet?"

Nick unrolled the floor plan less than a minute ago. "Not yet. We'll get him, Shane and then you can get Katie and go to Riley."

Shane stood, took up his favorite path and paced. He felt the rage tightening his nerve endings. If they didn't move soon, he'd snap. He wanted Domino more than he'd wanted anything in his life. Even Riley, and he wanted her bad. She was like a drug and the withdrawals of not feeling her hot tightness around him notched up his tension.

The doorbell rang. Shane opened it and stepped aside to allow Marc entrance.

"You ready to go?" he asked.

Nick didn't look up. "I may have found a way in."

Shane and Marc dropped to the floor and leaned over the floor plans of Domino's house. The massive stone structure sat on a two-acre lot right on the lake with a gated entrance and a high-tech security system. Both the boat house and dock were wired.

Nick found the security program in Domino's laptop and copied it. "This is our way in, if we can disable the alarm."

"If?" Shane raised his eyebrows and grinned. "You're kidding, right?"

Nick's expression turned serious and for a minute Shane wondered if his friend was telling the truth, but then he cracked and started laughing.

"Had you going, didn't I?"

"Dick."

"Relax, Shane." Nick smacked him in the shoulder as he stood and went down the hall. He returned with his laptop. "You're wound too tight. Why don't you go for a run? By the time you get back, I'll be ready to roll."

Marc stood. "Want some company?"

"Thanks, but you couldn't keep up."

"Try me."

Shane laughed. "Okay, you're on."

The first mile Shane kept pace with Marc, but once they hit the forest edge, Shane started to pull away. He ran another mile, then turned back and met up with Marc, who had decided to take a break.

Shane shook his head, laughing as he approached. "Sissy."

They ran in tandem on the way back and Marc actually kicked up the pace. Shane let him take a considerable lead before he turned on the jets, whizzing past Marc, who said something that sounded like "Fuck".

Marc was winded but laughing when he got back to the house and saw Shane kicked back in a chair, drinking a bottle of water.

Shane smiled and threw a bottle through the air. "Should've put money on our run. I could use the extra cash."

Marc caught the bottle with a grin. "You're a comedian, Blackstone."

"Yeah, I know. And Nick's a saint. He's ready to roll." Shane leaned forward, sucking down the last of the water. "I'll go get cleaned up and get my gear together while you fill Marc in." Shane said to Nick as he headed for a shower.

The run calmed him; he could now focus on taking Domino down. He needed to catch the fucker to prove he could be more than just a trained killer with no emotions, to save his sister, to avenge his parents. He needed to catch Domino so he could go after Riley and convince her to forgive him.

Jake called while on the road and had Shane scan the bug he found in Trevor's phone. It turned out to be a new high-tech device that wasn't detectable with a standard sweeper.

They'd only identified the thing in the last hour, when a techno-geek friend from the San Francisco office had called back to tell them where the device had come from.

Relief swept over him at the knowledge. When they'd swept Trevor and his car, he'd come up clean. There hadn't been any reason to be concerned, so Shane had taken every precaution he could have taken at the time. It wasn't much, but he hoped to hell Riley would stop blaming him.

Riley listened to her third message from Shane. The sound of his voice acted as a noose around her neck, tightened her throat until she couldn't breathe through the anguish.

She had fallen in love with him and he had killed her brother, used her to get him. And now she had to tell her parents.

She swiped at a tear as it dripped down her cheek. The sun tried to break through the fog as they crossed the Bay Bridge. They would be in her parents' driveway in under thirty minutes. Maybe they should just check into a hotel.

"Riley?" Beth broke into her thoughts. "You okay?"

Riley shook her head. She didn't think she would ever be okay again. Her heart was broken, she was about to break her parents' hearts.

Beth climbed into the back seat. She pulled Riley into her arms. "Get it out, Riley. You need to be strong for your parents. Go ahead and cry. Scream if you want to."

Tears flooded her eyes and Riley let them out. She cried until her eyes burned and until her head hurt. All the while, Beth handed her tissues and held on to her. A lifeline in a turbulent sea.

They were no longer moving. Riley looked out the window. Jake had pulled over near the Golden Gate Park. He sat quietly, staring out the front window.

"Thank you," she whispered, meeting his gaze in the rearview mirror. He nodded.

"I just need another minute." Riley turned away from Jake's watchful eyes and blew her nose.

Beth scooted away, reached down and handed Riley her purse.

Riley met her gaze over the bag and only then realized how selfish she had been. Beth watched Trevor die too and Riley hadn't even considered how it had affected her.

"Thank you, Beth." She took the bag. "Are you...?"

"Don't even ask. Let's just get through this."

She did the best she could to freshen up, but her eyes were beyond repair. Beth offered her a water-soaked napkin which Riley applied to her swollen eyes. It felt so good. She leaned her head back against the seat and let the cool, moist cloth refresh her. When the moisture was gone, she discarded the napkin and searched her overnight bag for her moisturizer.

Feeling as put back together as is possible in the backseat of the car after a horrific night and a long painful drive, she felt ready. Or as ready as she would ever be.

When they pulled in front of the yellow and white Victorian, Riley took a deep breath and stepped out of the car.

She stared up at the house she had lived in the latter part of her childhood and felt the tug of memories drag her down into a whirlpool of despair.

She couldn't go there.

She turned to Jake. "Thank you for everything."

"No need. Take care, Riley." He handed Riley her things and climbed back into the car.

"Are you ready?" Beth asked after saying her goodbyes to Jake.

Riley took a tentative step forward, "No."

The front door opened and Riley's stomach dropped.

"Riley, what on earth are you doing here?" Claudia Snow rushed down the stairs to greet her daughter. She threw her arms around Riley. "We got your message that something had come up, but why didn't you say you were..." Her mother stopped and looked at the car still at the curb. "Who's that?" Claudia looked from Riley to Beth and back to Riley.

"Let's go inside, Mom."

"Riley? What's wrong?" Her mother suddenly looked panicked.

Beth pulled the two women into the house and closed the door. Riley put her things down gently and then turned to her mother. "Where's Dad?"

"Out back. Riley, you're scaring me. What's happened?"

Riley fought to keep her tears at bay, surprised that she had more. She opened the back door and ran to her father. She threw her arms around his neck and held on for dear life.

"Hi, baby. What a nice surprise." He pulled her arms loose from his neck and held her away from him. One look and the tears broke free. "Riley?"

Beth joined them. "Hi, Stan. Can we go inside and sit down?"

Stan Snow was made of steel but at Beth's calm his shoulders turned in. He walked inside and took a seat at the kitchen table. Everyone else sat.

Riley took a deep breath. Without any idea how to soften the blow, she jumped right in the thick of it.

"Mom, Dad. I...there was a...Trevor is dead."

Her father stared at her, disbelief and shock warring in his expression.

Her mother made a sound that tore through Riley's soul.

Riley always felt as though her mother loved Trevor best. These last years had been very hard on everyone because Trevor had become so distant. But even when he was getting into trouble as a teen, their mother had been too accommodating, too forgiving.

Riley wondered what that kind of unconditional love felt like and she imagined that one could only feel that way about a child.

Stan Snow had been much more rigid. He loved Riley and Trevor fiercely, but he wasn't as forgiving with Trevor. They went several years without speaking which caused many fights.

Riley cringed as her mother sobbed. Stan jumped from his chair at Claudia's initial reaction and wrapped her tightly in his arms. Tears slipped down his cheeks as he held on to his wife.

Riley paced the kitchen, finally setting about the task of making tea. She couldn't explain just yet. She didn't know if she could explain at all.

Stan broke the silence. "How did it happen?"

Beth looked to Riley, who shook her head. She had to do this herself. "Trevor got mixed up with some crime lord named Domino." Riley went back to the table and took a seat. "He got in too deep and couldn't get out. He witnessed the murder of a couple and when he agreed to help convict Domino, he was -- we were sent to a safe place." Riley looked up from the table she'd been staring at. "Turned out that there was a bug of some sort in his phone and someone found us." She stopped, her voice cracking with emotion as the vision of Trevor popped into her head. "The window shattered," Riley began in a much softer voice. "And he...they shot him."

Shane slumped into the chair by the bedroom window. The shower hadn't offered much distraction. Quite the opposite. All he could think about was Riley and the need to hold her and comfort her.

His cell rang.

Jake.

"Talk to me. Is Riley okay?"

"Riley's with her parents. I imagine she's told them by now. Beth hasn't acknowledged her own shock yet. She called her boss and took a leave of absence. She's trying to be strong for Riley. I'm just coming through Vallejo, should be there in under three hours."

Shane took a deep breath, "Nick and I are working on a plan to get into Domino's house. Marc wants to be a part of it but we need to keep him away. Your timing should be just right. We need your help keeping Marc away from the illegal stuff." Marc would have the chance to take Domino down, but only after Shane and Nick did their thing.

"I'll handle Marc. See you in a few."

"Thanks for getting Riley there safely, Jake."

"No problem, bro."

Shane disconnected the call and leaned back in the chair. He squeezed his eyes closed. When his parents died, he'd been devastated. Shane couldn't fathom being in Riley's shoes right now. Having to pass on the news of Trevor's death, especially when he knew that Riley felt responsible. Because of him. He dragged her into this mess and even though Domino already had a hit out on Trevor, Riley would still blame Shane. He planned on convincing her to forgive him.

Somehow.

Determined, Shane finished packing his combat gear. He and Nick would plant the bugs in Domino's house, on his boat and in his cars -- all four of them. They would sit back and wait.

He found Nick studying the alarm system specifications. Marc, on the couch reading the paper. "You find our way into the rabbit hole yet?"

"Not entirely. But have no fear."

"Not for a second. Anybody hungry?"

Marc leapt off the sofa. "Thought you'd never ask."

"Right this way."

Shane and Marc whipped up a few sandwiches, grabbed three bottles of water and went back out to the living room.

"Got it!" Nick declared as Shane set his sandwich on the table beside the laptop.

"Thanks."

Nick picked up the sandwich and wolfed it down in four bites.

"Did you even taste that?" Marc asked.

"It was great." Nick opened the water, downed half of it and set it aside. "Okay, we disable the alarm on the section of fence by the boathouse first, then once I plant the virus, the system will go down in phases allowing us untraceable access through the entire compound."

"Brilliant," Shane said between bites. "How long will it take to write the virus program?"

"Hour or two." Nick answered as he punched at the keys. "Maybe Marc can go take a shower. He smells like a sweat shop."

"And leave you here to sneak off without me? Not a chance."

Shane sighed. "Marc, we've been over this. You can't go in. In fact, you know nothing about us going in. You'll get the anonymous phone call when the time comes. You make a career rocketing arrest. But you can't go in with us."

"I want the son-of-a-bitch before he goes after her. Not when." Marc had a personal stake in Domino's target and that made him dangerous, but Shane and Nick needed his help which is the only reason they told him that Domino's target was his Gina, Marc's ex, and the current Mayor of South Lake Tahoe who planned to shut down three of Domino's million dollar a year establishments.

"This isn't negotiable Marc. You stay here and wait for us. Period." Shane looked to Nick for support. Nick was busy writing his virus program, but for the quick flick of his thumb, there was no indication Nick was paying any attention to Marc and Shane at all.

Shane knew Nick was very aware of the situation. Nick intended on making sure Marc couldn't interfere. Shane nodded and went to his favorite chair. He picked up a book and lost himself in it while the computer keys clattered.

The sound of a door slamming had Shane on his feet. Jake walked in before Shane got to the door. He looked at his watch, "Impressive. Two hours and thirty-eight minutes."

Jake threw him the car keys. "Nice ride." He went straight to the kitchen and returned with a bottle of water. "Hey Marc."

"Jake, how are you?"

"Good. Did you get the mess at my house cleaned up?"

"Yeah. You might need to replace the carpet but the window is fixed."

"Thanks. We ready to move?"

Nick stopped typing, "Not quite." His gaze traveled to Marc.

Jake looked from Nick to Shane, then to Marc. His expression filled with understanding. Jake moved toward his friend and put an arm around his shoulder. Shane left the room, knowing Marc would prefer to leave without an audience.

Jake, Marc and Shane had been friends for a long time. They would defend without question, hesitation or judgment. Most of all, they shared a mutual respect only achieved through years of friendship. Marc would leave without a scene and thank them later for protecting him.

Shane sat down in the chair in his bedroom, staring at the bed, thinking of Riley. He wouldn't call her again, he decided. Hard as it would be, he would wait until Domino was either dead or in jail, then he would go to Riley and make things right.

He pulled his cell from his pocket and punched in Dr. Banks' number. After the third ring, Shane's gut twisted with fear.

"Hello," she answered on a rush of air.

"It's Shane. You okay?"

"Shane. Yes. I just came in from a run."

"How's Katie?"

"She's up and in good spirits. We talked last night and I think she's had a breakthrough. She's remembering details about the night of your parents' death."

"Will she be able to handle it when she does remember?" Shane feared she would go deeper into herself when the memories came.

"It's hard to know, Shane. I believe she will cope with the grief and the guilt. The reason she hasn't remembered is because she's blocking out the truth in order to cope."

"I get it. When she can handle the truth, she'll allow herself to remember?"

"Pretty much, yes."

"I hope I can be there for her when that happens. In the meantime. We're about to make a move and I need to know the two of you are safe."

"We're fine. Good luck, Shane."

"I'll be there as soon as this is over."

"See you then."

Shane disconnected the call and leaned back in his chair. God willing, he would be there for Katie. He wanted this done. Now.

He walked back to the living room as Nick put his laptop into its bag. "We're ready to go."

"Marc okay?" he asked Jake.

Jake nodded. "He already knew we wouldn't let him go."

"Figured that, but he was chomping at the bit." Shane dragged a hand through his lengthening hair. "Wouldn't be so bad if it wasn't his ex."

Jake shook his head, "You mean the woman he wants to win back."

"No shit?" Shane knew that Marc and Gina had a rocky history, but they kept getting back together and with each reunion came a more explosive break-up.

"Jenna talked them into counseling. They've been going for about three weeks."

"Son-of-a-bitch. Why didn't he say something?" Shane couldn't imagine how hard this must be on Marc, although he was closer to imagining than he'd ever been before. Because of Riley.

"You know how Marc plays things close to the vest."

"Yeah. I do." Shane said to Nick's retreating back as he headed down the hall to change.

Nick came back into the room, dressed in black fatigues, a long-sleeved black t-shirt and black boots. "You ready?"

"Damn straight." Shane checked his back holster for his favored Glock. "Let's get this done."

Chapter Seventeen

Riley barely slept. She had taken a nap after her mom fell asleep. Her father had convinced her mom to lie down and then he disappeared outside. Beth and Riley shared Riley's room. She was grateful for her support and even though Riley had tried to convince Beth to go home to her own parents, Beth insisted on staying.

Three cups of strong coffee and a piece of toast hadn't helped Riley but she forced herself to get ready for the dreadful day ahead. She dressed in clothing to match her mood: a pair of dark grey slacks and a light grey turtleneck, with a black leather jacket and black boots.

Light rain dripped from the sky, darkening Riley's mood further.

Shane called three times the first day, but hadn't called since. Not that she wanted to talk to him, but somewhere deep down inside she hoped he'd tried harder.

After dropping Beth at her own parents' house, she and her mom went to a local flower shop.

Riley parked the car. She reached for the door handle but realized her mom hadn't moved. Riley touched her arm, "You ready?"

Her mother sniffed. "I can't do this, Riley."

"Oh, Mom." Riley leaned over the center console and hugged her mother. "I'm so sorry. I can't imagine how hard this is for you."

Her mom shook as she cried in Riley's arms.

Riley cried too. For her Mother. For the pain she had inflicted on her family. How could she have allowed Shane to tuck Trevor away. She should have forced him to let the police protect him or put him in witness protection or whatever the hell they did with a witness.

Her mom stopped crying and was now patting Riley's back gently. "I know you're upset too, Riley." She pulled away, sniffled again and wiped her tears with a tissue she pulled from her purse. "I'm sure it was just horrible for you and Beth."

Riley couldn't respond. How could she? She was alive. Trevor wasn't.

"Come on. Let's go get this done." Her mom opened her door and climbed from the car. Riley knew her mom was being brave for Riley's sake but her heart must be shattered.

They walked arm and arm into the flower shop. A young woman with long black hair and big brown eyes smiled at them. "May I help you?"

"We need to pick out flowers for a funeral." Riley offered.

"I'm so sorry for your loss." Then the woman snatched a box of tissue from underneath the counter and walked over to a small table. "Have a seat," she said, setting the box in the center. "I'll just grab a few books from the back and join you in a second."

"Thank you," Riley answered.

"My name is Liz." She set the books down and pulled a rolling chair over to the table.

"I'm Riley. This is my mother, Claudia."

Liz clearly knew her job. She gave Riley a sympathetic look and then turned to her mom. "Claudia, do you have anything specific in mind?"

"No. I...no."

"May I ask who passed?"

Claudia sighed. "My son." She pulled a tissue from the box and dabbed at her eyes.

"Where will you hold the service?" Liz asked gently.

"First Lutheran on 50th." Riley responded.

Liz opened a book and flipped through several pages, settling on one, she turned the book around so it faced Riley's mom.

Claudia looked at the pictures and shook her head.

Liz turned the page, waited, then turned another one.

"Can we do something more colorful?" Claudia whispered. "I don't want anything formal. I'm thinking maybe Trevor would like something masculine and bright."

Liz took her book away and returned with a book filled with unusual wildflowers. Claudia flipped through the pages herself and settled on a page of masculine but beautiful arrangements.

Liz asked more questions, made notes on her pad and reached beneath the table for another book. This one filled with samples of stationary.

Tears pooled in Riley's eyes again as she watched her mother sift through the many choices.

"What color is appropriate for announcing the death of a child?" The tone was Riley's undoing and she ran from the store, into the rain.

She looked down the sidewalk, wanting refuge but finding none. A touch on her shoulder dragged her attention from her grief, it was so soft.

"I'm sorry, dear. I didn't mean anything by that. I just don't know what to do."

Riley turned to her beautiful, wonderful mother, "I'm so sorry. If I hadn't gotten involved with Shane, this never would have happened." Riley hadn't mentioned Shane. But the guilt gnawed at her like a rat on a rope.

"Whatever do you mean by that?"

Rain drops mixed with tears as Riley explained how she met Shane. How he intentionally pursued her to get the goods on Trevor. When she finished, a sense of relief swamped her as a sob tore from her chest.

"You can hate me for my culpability but I swear we tried to help in the end."

Claudia Snow very calmly led Riley back into the store. Liz went into the back, returning with a towel. Riley dropped onto a stool. Her mother, with heartbreaking love in her eyes patted Riley's face dry, wiping a smudge of mascara carefully from beneath her eye.

"It's not your fault, Riley. I don't blame you. And I don't blame Shane, though we will talk more about him later." Riley almost smiled at her mother's inference. "Trevor was in trouble long before you moved to Tahoe. Don't think for a second that your father and I didn't know what kind of hoodlums he ran with. We don't blame you."

Riley felt fresh tears threatened to erupt. "I love you." Riley hugged her mother.

"I love you too dear. Now let's get this done and get home." Claudia went back to the table. "Then you can tell me about Shane."

"Oh, Mom."

"Don't 'Oh, Mom' me. I want all the sorted details. I've seen the light the lit your eyes with the mention of his name. Or the darkness. This is serious, isn't it?"

"It's over. There's nothing to tell."

A smile split her mother's face. "Right." She turned to the kind woman who had been sensitive enough to give them privacy, "I think we'll go with the gray silk announcements."

As soon as they were settled in the car, Riley's phone rang. She made no move to answer it.

"Why are you ignoring him, Riley?"

Finally, she pulled the phone from her purse, pushed the talk button, "Hey Beth." Relief and disappointment battled in her heart.

"How are you and Claudia doing?"

"We're finished with the arrangements and heading home." Riley wasn't looking forward to an afternoon of doing nothing. It would allow her too much time to dwell on her feelings for Shane.

"What do you think about meeting me at the wharf for an afternoon of tourism?"

Riley looked out at the cloudy sky. The rain had let up and bits of blue peeked through. Exactly what Riley needed. "Sounds great. Where and when?"

"Are you hungry?"

"Starved." Riley's stomach grumbled its agreement, though she didn't feel like eating she knew she needed to keep up her strength.

"Okay, then. Let's meet at Fog City Diner in thirty."

"Yum! See you there." Riley dropped her phone in the slot inside her purse. She turned to her mother, "Beth wants to do lunch at Fog City, then play at the wharf this afternoon. You up for it?"

Hesitation flashed briefly, "I could use some girl time and your dad needs his space. He's taking this hard. He blames himself for Trevor's getting involved with that Domino guy. Trevor asked for help and your father refused. He told him to grow a backbone and be a man."

Riley patted her mother's arm. "Are you sure you should leave him alone."

"It's how he deals with his emotions, Riley. I need to hear about the joy in your life. It softens the pain for me. Now let's get going."

Riley pulled into traffic. "Thanks, Mom."

"For what?"

"Not blaming me."

Traffic slogged through town but Riley made it to the Diner in less than thirty minutes. She even found a parking space two blocks up from the trendy restaurant.

Fog City Diner hadn't changed since Riley's last trip to San Francisco. The 50's style décor beefed up with trendy modernism was fun and hip. The oysters and the clam chowder were the best in the area. Even better than the Grotto on the wharf. Riley's mouth watered just looking at the menu.

"What do you think about sharing some appetizers and a couple of entrees?" Riley couldn't make up her mind what she wanted. One of everything sounded good to her. Suddenly her appetite kicked into high gear.

"Works for me. But what we need first is wine." Beth decided. "Be right back."

Riley watched Beth weave through the crowd to the bar. She leaned over and whispered in the very *HOT* bartenders' ear.

Beth came back, grinning from ear to ear. "Watch out Riley. The bartender, whose name is Steve, thinks you're gorgeous and is bringing over a special bottle of wine."

"Yeah, right." Riley smacked Beth's arm. "I think he's hot for you. His smile is terrific though. How old do you think he is?"

"Thirty-two," the deep voice came from behind her.

Riley felt her face flush. She turned, as Steve set a bottle of Rombauer on the table.

"And thanks for the compliment." He smiled again and Riley noticed the dimples etched in each cheek. Yes, he was quite adorable.

He opened the bottle, splashed a taste into a glass and handed it to Riley. She sampled the wine, nodded and handed her glass back to him so he could fill it.

"Your waiter will be over in a second to take your order." He winked at Riley and returned to the bar.

Riley turned to her mother, embarrassed by the whole exchange. "Sorry, Mom."

"For what?" Claudia said as she watched her daughter.

"For flirting and carrying on when we're supposed to be..." Riley had no idea how to finish her sentence. Planning Trevor's funeral? Grieving for a son and brother?

"We aren't dead, Riley. Trevor is. We can't change it and life goes on." Claudia grinned, but Riley noticed the effort if took. "Besides, he is quite handsome."

"Hot, Mom. He's Hot." Riley answered.

"So is Shane." Beth stated flatly.

At the reminder of Shane, Riley's attention left Steve. "Let's not go there, Beth."

"No lets." Claudia Snow was not about to let her daughter throw away a chance at happiness. The conversations she'd had with her daughter over the last couple of weeks, even though not specifically about Shane had been filled with joy.

"Mom, I don't want to talk about Shane."

To Riley's relief, the waiter appeared and took their order of oysters on the half shell, clam chowder, salad and crab cakes. He topped off their wine and left.

"Now spill," Claudia ordered.

"Mother. Don't push."

Beth laughed. "I'll fill you in on all the sinful details."

"Please do."

"Beth. Knock it off." Riley knew she couldn't keep this from her mother. She was in love with Shane. Madly and deeply. But they couldn't be together now. End of story.

Beth replayed the night they'd met Shane in vivid detail, then Riley took over and told her about their first date, leaving out the part about the room and the wild sex of course. She explained Shane's confession about their chance meeting and how Riley had agreed to help him. Finally, she told her about Trevor's death.

"And how is Trevor's death Shane's fault? Though I would love to blame somebody." Claudia sighed, then straightened and continued. "Seems to me he was trying to protect Trevor. He gave him a chance to do the right thing and Trevor took it. I think you should be grateful that Shane tried to help him instead of blaming him."

Riley stared at her mother. Shocked. Awed. Touched.

"I know Trevor was mixed up with some bad people, Riley. His home was filled with things he couldn't afford on a bouncer's salary. He was secretive and defensive. I already told you how he stole from us to help pay his debts." Claudia took a sip of wine. "You clearly love Shane. Why are you pushing him away?"

Why? Because she was terrified. She trusted him to protect them all and she could've died too. A snapshot of Trevor's lifeless body scrolled through her mind followed by one of her cheating ex. She was afraid. Afraid to trust. Afraid to really let herself love him. "I don't know, Mom."

The food arrived, giving Riley a chance to redirect the conversation. "So, Beth. What's up with you and Nick?"

Beth swallowed the oyster she had just slid into her mouth, "I'm not sure yet, but I am looking forward to seeing him as soon as they arrest Domino."

Beth had talked to Nick several times since they'd arrived in The City. Beth explained the evidence he and Shane found, that they had planted bugs in Dominico's home and were just waiting for him to make his move.

"Nick said it should all be over in a couple of days."

"Thank God." Riley and Claudia said in unison.

They finished their meal, waved goodbye to Steve and headed out into the crisp afternoon. Riley dug her sunglasses out of her purse. As they walked to the wharf, she thought about what her mother said. Of course, she was right. Shane tried to help. It wasn't his fault.

But could Riley push aside her fear? Should she dare to live her truth? Loving Shane had brought so much joy to her life.

Chapter Eighteen

S hane spread the newspaper out on the kitchen table. The front page filled with the arrest of Joseph 'Domino' Dominico. He read the article for the fourth time.

He had expected a sense of satisfaction. Instead he felt empty and alone. He knew they couldn't go into detail about Domino's guilt in the paper or the news but still...

His parents died because his father discovered Domino's fetish for young girls. The evidence his father gathered would not have been enough to convict the scumbag. That's what really hurt. They died for nothing.

The attempt on Regina Hiroshi failed thanks to Jake, who had taken out the would-be-assassin before the kill orders were even issued.

Riley hadn't returned his calls but he knew she was okay because Nick talked to Beth. Trevor's body had been released and the funeral was scheduled for tomorrow. Shane planned to be there. He would hold Riley's hand whether she liked it or not.

The front door slammed. "Shane? You here?" Nick asked coming into the kitchen. "You ready?"

They were due to pick up Katie in an hour, then they would continue over the mountain to San Francisco. Nick would take Katie sightseeing while Shane attended the service.

"Ready."

Together, they locked the house. Light snow fell from the darkening sky. "Think we can beat the storm?"

Nick smiled. "It's coming in from the south. We'll be fine."

"Something funny?" Shane asked as Nick backed out of the drive.

"You're nervous," he answered with a widening grin.

Nervous didn't begin to describe it. "Shove it."

Nick laughed. "You do have it bad, don't you?"

Now Shane smiled. "I do."

The drive to Incline Village on the North Shore of Lake Tahoe took thirty-five minutes. Nick drove in silence for a time, giving Shane a chance to close his eyes. It had been a long couple of days.

When Shane finally sat up and focused on the road again, Nick asked, "How do you plan to win her back?"

Shane didn't flinch at the question. He expected it. But he didn't have a plan past being present, beside Riley during the funeral.

"You don't have a plan?"

Nick's questions burned because ideas flitted around like mosquitoes in the swamp, unfortunately none landed.

"You gotta have a plan, Shane." Nick stated in his best, are you out of your mind you idiot tone.

"Okay, hot shot. What would you do?"

Nick thought for a minute as Shane turned his attention back to the road and to Nick's point. He did need a plan. Shane had considered flowers, candy, all the normal romancing and/or apologizing clichés. They all seemed trite. Shane wanted something special, something big. Nothing came to mind.

"Why not try the truth?"

Shane fought the urge to laugh. He already tried that in the three voice messages he left. "I tried that already. She either didn't listen to my messages or chose to ignore them."

Nick sighed. "You told her you loved her in a message?"

"No. I explained the tracking device and --"

"Dammit Shane. You can't try to reason with her in a message. She needs to hear you say you love her, that you want to marry her, that you can't live without her." He shook his head.

Marry her? Was he kidding? Crazy about her? Yes. In love with her? Honestly?

Yes.

Nick slapped his friend on the shoulder. "You need to tell her."

The rest of the ride to Incline went quickly as Shane sifted through various scenarios of how he would tell her how he felt. He already told her loved her. But she hadn't responded and Shane wondered if it had to do with the fact that he had just fucked her.

Truth be told, Shane loved her and had to tell her. For real. Now that his parents' death was avenged, he needed to make some decisions about his future. Funny thing, he couldn't imagine any scenarios without Riley in them.

Shane only realized they had arrived at Katie's safe house when Nick shoved him out of his internal strategy session. He climbed from the car, still deep in thought.

They walked down the hallway toward Katie's room just as Dr. Banks emerged.

"Just in time," Dr. Banks said with a smile. "Katie's ready to go. She's remembered everything and she's going to be okay, Shane."

Relief washed over him. He hugged the doctor, surprising them both. "Thank you."

"You're quite welcome. I would like to continue seeing her but I really believe that aside from some understandable bouts of depression she'll be fine. Keep her busy, talk about what happened and don't mollycoddle her."

"Got it." Shane thanked her again, then walked into Katie's room.

"Shane!" Katie jumped from the bed and threw herself at Shane. He held her in a long hug.

"How are you Katiedid?"

"I'm okay. They told me you caught the bastard who killed our parents."

Shane sucked in a breath at the vehemence in her voice. "We did." He chose to ignore her poor language. Although he would've used a much stronger word.

"Good." She let go of Shane, stepping away to get her things.

"What do you think about a trip the City?" Shane would tell her about Trevor and Riley on the way.

She hesitated as if she sensed something amiss.

"I'll explain on the way."

"Okay, I guess." Katie headed toward the door. "Is Riley here?"

"No. Nick is though."

Katie continued out of room. Shane smiled as Nick greeted Katie. They had gotten close over the last few months.

He joined them in the hall. "Let's get this party started."

Nick took the wheel again, this time so that Shane could fill Katie in on the details of Domino's arrest, then he told her about Trevor.

"Oh my God." Katie's expression became haunted, her complexion paled. "He's the one who saved me."

"He what?" Nick and Shane shared the same shocked reaction.

"He pushed me out the way just before the blast. I thought he was the one who caused it, but he tried to save me."

Thunderstruck, Shane looked to Nick, then back at Katie. "He saved you?"

"Yes." Katie whispered. "Poor Riley." Katie reached over the seat and put her hand on Shane's shoulder. "I'm sorry, Shane."

"Thanks," he patted her hand. "She's pretty angry at me, but maybe when she finds out that he..." Shane couldn't finish his sentence. He realized the truth might just cause her to place even more blame at his feet.

"I don't mind getting out of town. I'm not really looking forward to going home anyway."

Shane hadn't expected that.

Katie continued, "I remember everything Shane but I'm not ready to face walking through the front door just yet." She stared out the window for a long time. "At least they didn't suffer. I think I blocked out the night to stave off the guilt."

Shane turned and watched Katie swipe at the tears on her cheeks. She closed her eyes, took a calming breath. Shane focused on the front windshield again. He understood the need to face demons. He dealt with it every day, so he waited for Katie to continue, thankful that she remembered and could now deal with the pain and anger.

"I think Riley is good for you, Shane. I hope you can work things out."

Shocked by her words, but surprisingly pleased at the same time, he smiled. "Thanks, kiddo. I hope so too." The snow continued to blanket the Sierras as Nick drove through Donner Pass. "What do you think about a vacation?" Shane decided in a split second that Hawaii would be a great place to transition Katie back into her life without their parents. And maybe maneuver Riley into his.

"Really?" Katie's smile was huge and sincere. "I'd love to go to Hawaii."

"Me too," Nick's playful response made Shane laugh.

"Okay, you can come too."

"What about Riley? Can we invite her?" Katie must have read his mind. Creepy.

"Great idea." Shane grinned. "Maybe Beth will join us."

Nick stared straight ahead into the snowy twilight, pretending to focus on the road.

"Nick?" Nick threw a quick glance in Shane's direction. "Sure," he answered without enthusiasm.

Shane didn't fall for Nick's feigned indifference. He had seen the spark between the two. So why did Nick hesitate? "Why are you sitting on the fence when it comes to Beth?"

Nick didn't answer right away.

"Yeah," Katie added.

"Not looking for anything serious." Nick's tone indicated the end of the discussion.

Shane had other ideas. "You really like her, don't you?"

"Leave it alone, Shane."

Shane grinned. "Whatever you say."

Nick leveled him with a deadly stare.

Shane laughed from deep down in his gut. When he could talk, he simply said, "That bad, huh."

Nick flipped him the bird and Shane and Katie laughed.

They had gone far enough down the mountain that the snow turned to rain. The darkness seemed deeper too. Shane leaned back and closed his eyes.

He dreamed of Riley, lurid, sexy, forbidden dreams that had him anxious and aroused when he awoke.

Shane stretched, adjusting the bulge in his pants. Katie slept peacefully in the backseat. The Bay Bridge lit up the night and the lights of San Francisco twinkled like a trillion stars. Shane's stomach did a cartwheel at the idea that he would see Riley in a few hours.

The clock on the dash read 12:18. By the time they settled into their hotel room, he'd only have a couple hours of sleep before seeing her.

"You okay?" he asked Nick.

"Fine. It's been an easy, uneventful drive."

"Did you come to terms with your feelings for Beth in the silence?" Shane couldn't help but goad Nick.

"Fuck you."

"Come on, Nick. I got it bad for Riley. I'm terrified. I think staring down the enemy was less scary, but I think...no, I know I am in love with her. Ready or not."

Nick gripped the wheel tighter. "I'm not in love with Beth, but I feel like I could easily fall. I don't want to go there."

"Why not?"

"Because it's suffocating and debilitating and takes all of my energy to keep from thinking about her. My dick is hard all the time and I feel like I'm gonna drown."

"It's got you already, Nick. Just go with it. You might be surprised where it takes you."

Shane had already been down this road. He'd tried to convince himself that he would never be good enough for Riley. That he didn't deserve her. That he would let her down like everyone else in his life. But he was working on changing that. He had saved Katie, hadn't he?

"I'll invite her to Hawaii with us and we'll see where it goes. But if it doesn't work out, I might feel the need to kick the shit out of you."

Shane and Nick both laughed the rest of the way to their hotel. Katie woke, asked what was funny and set them off all over again.

The rain that had fallen all night continued into the morning. Shane went for a run from the Embarcadero Hotel where they stayed, down to Pier 39 and back.

Nick and Katie were still asleep. They planned to spend the day at the very Pier Shane had just passed by. He took a long hot shower, mentally reviewing what he would say to Riley after she pummeled him. He dressed in a black suit with gray pinstripes, a gray shirt and a plum tie. He climbed into his car, following directions from his GPS to Riley's parents' home.

He pulled up in front of the Victorian and took a deep breath, steeling himself for the onslaught of anger and accusation Riley would surely throw his way.

Be patient with her. Be there for her.

It would be his mantra all day, or at least until she forgave him.

He climbed from the car. With determined focus he went up the walk, climbed the stairs to the front door, then knocked before he could chicken out.

An auburn-haired woman answered the door dressed in a long-sleeved black sheath. Eyes shaped liked Riley's stared at him.

"You must be Mrs. Snow?" Shane asked gently.

She nodded. "Claudia. And I'm guessing you're Shane."

"I am." Shane expected Riley's mother to slam the door in his face.

"Please come in." she stepped aside, allowing him entry into a foyer with an antique coat rack and table. "I'm not sure how welcome you'll be but I'm glad you're here."

Taken aback, Shane looked into Claudia's sad eyes. "Thank you."

"Riley's in the kitchen. I'll show you the way and leave you to talk." True to her word, Claudia took Shane down a short hallway, pointed to the door at the end, then turned into a sitting room.

Shane pushed the door open slowly, wishing he had a white hanky to announce his presence. Riley looked up from the newspaper she'd been reading, clearly shocked to see Shane standing there. At first her eyes flashed with happiness, but they quickly dimmed as anger took its place.

"What are you doing here, Shane?" She stood, crossing her arms over her chest.

Her black blouse hugged her breasts, flaring below them over her waist. Her skirt dropped inward toward her boot clad feet. She looked even more beautiful than the sensual creature he had dreamt about every night since he'd met her.

But there was a sadness in her eyes that broke his heart into a million tiny pieces.

He moved toward her, put his hands on her shoulders. His gaze never wavered from hers. "I'm here to offer you support and comfort."

She sucked in a breath, obviously surprised by his frankness.

"Please go." She actually looked down at the floor.

"No. I won't go. You can ignore me all day if you want but I will be here, beside you, to hold your hand, or be your shoulder."

Her gaze darted back to Shane's, shock and something else darkening her irises.

Minutes passed, neither moved. Finally, Shane pulled her close and hugged her. She stiffened at the initial contact then melted into him like butter on toast. Her arms came around him, her head dropped to his chest. He relaxed, releasing breath he hadn't realized he'd been holding.

After a time, she pushed away, "I can't talk about this today, but thank you for coming." She brushed past him leaving him alone in the room with only her lingering scent.

He had hoped she would yell at him or hit him or something, that he could respond to, but thanking him and calmly walking away? What the fuck was he supposed to do with that.

He sat down at the table and waited.

The kitchen, painted a lively shade of green felt dreary when coupled with the gray drizzle of the morning and Shane's confused mood. He waited for several minutes, expecting Riley to return for him, instead Claudia came into the room.

"Didn't go well, did it?" She rinsed the coffee cup she carried into the room with her and put it in the stainless dishwasher.

"Not so much," Shane answered with a frown.

"She's trying not to blame you for her brother's death." Claudia pulled out a chair across from him, sitting down on a sigh. "By the way, I don't blame you."

Surprised, Shane reached across the table, putting his hand on top of hers. "Thank you."

"Trevor was always in trouble of one kind or another. I think Riley feels a bit of responsibility in this but it's easier to blame you. She had her heart ripped out a couple of times already and you have her running scared, terrified actually," she smiled. "Hang in there. At the end of the day, she'll be glad you were by her side through this, even though she's trying very hard to push you away."

He understood the terrified part. He wanted to tear the throats out of the people who had 'ripped her heart out'. The strength of his possessiveness, and the protectiveness he felt toward Riley compared to nothing he had experienced before.

"I will be here for her. Thank you."

"You're welcome." She stood, "Stan's got the car warming," her voice had become sad again and Shane felt his heart clench.

"Then we should go." He put his arm out to escort her from the room. "You are a gentleman. What a pleasant surprise."

Shane grinned, "Not always."

Claudia chuckled, "Now that I believe."

They walked down the hall to the foyer. The front door stood open, the small crowd on the porch moved down the steps when they appeared. Shane checked the lock before closing the door tightly.

He caught up with Riley. "Please ride with me."

She shook her head, climbing into the car with her parents.

"I'll come with you," Beth offered with a small smile.

He nodded, went to his car to open the door for her.

"She's trying really hard to stay mad at you," Beth said when they pulled away from the curb, "but she'll get over it."

Shane ran through the days' mantra again.

Beth shifted in her seat. "How's Nick?"

Shane glanced her way. "He's good. He and Katie are cruising the Pier today."

"Huh," Beth answered.

Shane should keep his mouth shut given the predicament between he and Riley, he couldn't let Beth suffer. "We're having dinner at Flint's Landing tonight. "You and Riley should join us."

Beth sat up straighter, hope bright in her eyes. "Really?"

"It's one of my favorite restaurants. We thought maybe we'd even take the ferry over if the weather gets better."

"I'm not sure Riley will want to leave her mom and dad so soon after the service, but we'll see." Beth rattled off instructions to the church. "How's Katie doing?"

"She's good. She's remembered everything. Beth, Trevor saved her life?"

"What?" Beth shouted. "Oh my God, Shane. You have to tell Riley and her parents. They need to know he wasn't all bad." Beth stared out the window for a time. As they pulled into the church parking lot, she turned back to Shane. "Why didn't he tell us?"

"I don't know," Shane said as he parked under a big oak tree.

The rain had let up, the clouds parting enough to allow the blue sky to peek through so Shane and Beth waited in silence for everyone outside.

The trip to the church passed in a blink. Riley's thoughts never left the memory of Shane; the sight of him in his suit set her insides on fire.

He smelled of pine and soap and man. She'd pushed away from him to keep her sanity, because what she'd really wanted...

"Riley?" her mother's voice dragged her attention from her thoughts.

Riley looked out the window. Shane and Beth stood near the church steps talking. Beth smiled. Shane glanced toward the car and Riley shifted her gaze to the doorknob.

Suck it up. Head high. And don't get too close.

Shane opened the door for her.

When had he moved?

His hand appeared. Riley took it, the contact ignited the already smoldering burn of desire.

Riley shivered.

Shane squeezed her hand.

As soon as she stood up fully, she released his hand, breaking contact. Distance is the only way she would survive.

She headed toward Beth, her lifeline.

Together they went into the church and took seats in the front row. Shane sat beside her. She sent him a glaring look, but he only smiled and reached for her hand. She took it, seething with -- frustration. He knew how he affected her, yet he continued to touch her. He leaned in, "It's okay, Red. I know you're mad and I know you can't stop the desire curling through your blood. I'm here, whatever you need."

She ripped her hand from his grip. He laughed. He actually laughed, damn him. She tried to scoot away, closer to Beth, but her friend-turned-traitor didn't budge. Shane slid over so that their thighs touched.

A jolt of electricity burned through her, straight to her clitoris. *Oh My God! I'm in a church, for my brother's funeral and all I can think about is Shane's hands on me.*

She swatted his hand away when he tried to rest it on her thigh.

Everyone quieted as the minister approached the podium. Suddenly Shane's presence became a comfort. She felt his strength emanating from his pores. She focused on the strength he offered, forcing her desire away. Or at least trying to.

When the service ended, they walked to the gravesite and watched as the coffin was lowered into the ground. A shovel of dirt thrown on top, another prayer and then the procession of people dropping a single rose into the hole ending the ceremony.

Again, with Shane beside her, Riley cried. The time came to head back to her parents' house and Shane asked her to ride with him. She agreed this time, surprising them both.

Shane didn't start the car after they'd buckled up, instead he turned to her. "I'm so sorry, Riley."

Tears threatened, not for Trevor this time, but for her and Shane. He waited, expecting her to say something. She remained silent. He sighed, starting the car.

They were halfway back to her house when she spoke. "I know you tried to help Trevor," she swallowed, fighting back the sob that threatened. "But I can't see you anymore." Riley swiped at the tears that dripped down her cheeks. "I can't help but think that he'd be alive if I hadn't gotten involved with you." She dug in her purse, extracting a tissue. She dabbed at her eyes.

Shane felt the crack of each rib as his chest was splayed open and his heart torn out. He sucked in a breath, hoping to ease the ache.

Riley took a deep breath, "I appreciate that you were here today, but it would be better if you'd drop me at home and go," her voice almost inaudible when she finished.

That was it? End of story?

Hell no!

Shane would honor her wishes for now, but he wouldn't let go. Her mother's words played in his mind, 'At the end of the day she'll be glad you were here for her' didn't make him feel any better but somehow gave him the strength to respect her wishes.

He wanted to fight for her. Wanted to tell her he loved her.

He didn't.

He pulled up to the curb, got out, opened her door, and helped her from the car.

"I need to talk to you. And your parents."

"Why?" Riley didn't want him to stay. It hurt too much.

"Trust me," Shane winced at his choice of words. "It's important, Riley."

"This really isn't a good time Shane."

"There will never be a good time, Riley. But this is important. There's something you all need to know."

The front door opened and Riley's father stepped onto the porch. Shane started to pull her toward the house.

"No. Not now." Riley hissed as he gripped her hand tighter and climbed the steps to the porch.

He dropped Riley's hand and reached out toward her father. "Mr. Snow. I am deeply sorry for your loss."

"Thank you. Shane, I presume?"

"Yes, sir." Shane straightened, glanced at Riley and continued, "If you have a moment, I would like to speak with you and your wife. I realize it isn't the best time, but it is very important."

Her father looked to her with sadness in his eyes. Riley could only shrug her shoulders in answer. She didn't want to be near Shane. Didn't want to hear what he had to say.

"Certainly, come in."

Riley's heart continued to break as her father directed them to the study. "I'll get your Mother."

Shane stopped his pacing when Riley's parents entered the study. The door closed with a click and Riley shivered at the nerves skittering throughout her body. She watched Shane settle into the chair across from her parents. Riley chose to remain standing behind the couch where her parents sat.

"Thank you for giving me a few minutes. I know this day is very difficult for you. I wanted to let you know that I am truly sorry for not doing a better job of protecting your son. I will carry this guilt with me until the day I die. I learned last night that your son actually saved my sister from dying the day my parents were killed."

Riley nearly choked from the shock of his words.

"Trevor had been following my parents that night at the orders of Domino. He admitted that to us, but for some reason neglected to tell us that he had been there to try to stop the hit on my family." Shane looked at Riley, the pain in his gaze causing tears to well in her eyes. "It was too late for my parents, but he managed to push my sister Katie into the house and away from the explosion just in time. Katie assumed he had been the one to cause the explosion. Her shock at watching our parents die skewed her perception of things. But she has remembered everything. She wanted you to know the truth, Riley."

Tears rolled down Riley's cheeks. He wanted so badly to go to her and pull her into his arms, but Shane didn't reach for her. His heart pounding in his chest, he stood.

Claudia and Stan stood as well.

Stan reached out a hand to Shane. "Thank you."

Tears filled Claudia's eyes as she stepped around the coffee table. She gave Shane a quick hug. "It wasn't your fault Shane. You didn't know." The tears she'd been holding let go and her husband reached into his pocket and pulled a small packet of tissues out, handing it to his wife. "You tried to help him. I will always be grateful to you for that."

"You're too kind, Mrs. Snow." Shane glanced at Riley, who turned away.

"I'd best be getting back to my sister." Shane said as his heart broke.

No one stopped him as he left and he wondered if he would ever see Riley again. She looked so hurt. So angry. So torn.

And that look of longing, of wanting him even though she blamed him, gave him a splinter of hope.

Chapter Nineteen

"Are you out of your mind?" Beth shouted. "He's the best thing that's ever happened to you." Beth paced the front porch. "Ever."

She met Riley in the foyer and pushed her back outside, forcing her to explain why Shane left. Riley had never seen her so furious. Well, she'd seen Beth fuming, raging angry, just never aimed at Riley.

Her friend dropped into one of the wicker chairs, crossing her arms over her chest.

Waiting.

Riley stared at her, stunned. What could she say? Shane treated her with love and respect. He knew how to please a woman. His looks could land him on the cover of most magazines. Strong. Protective. Honest? Reliable? Loyal?

"Well?" Beth asked, clearly not planning to let the subject drop.

The pressure and indecision of the last week churned in her stomach, threatening to erupt. Riley wanted to scream, wanted to stomp her feet and pitch a fit. Instead she laughed.

Beth's response went from shock to concern.

Riley sat down in the chair beside her friend. When her laughter subsided, she lowered her head into her hands.

Looking up, she turned toward Beth. "I'm crazy in love with him."

Beth waited. Riley wanted her to say something, anything. Her friend remained silent.

"He told me Trevor would be okay," she said, imploring Beth to agree. "He lied. I can't do it again. Saying goodbye is the best for both of us."

"Why?"

"Because. I can't trust him." Riley didn't, wouldn't continue.

"You can't trust him? He tried to help Trevor. It wasn't his fault Trevor died. Shane isn't the one who ordered Trevor's death and he didn't pull the trigger." Beth leaned in and grasped Riley's hands in hers, looking her square in the eyes. "I think your problem is that you can't trust yourself."

Riley couldn't lie. "Maybe I'm afraid I'll do something to disappoint him and he'll find someone else. Just like Robert did."

Now Beth laughed. The sound hollow, gritty. "You didn't do anything to deserve -- or more importantly encourage Robert to cheat. He did it. Him." Beth took a deep breath, releasing her grip.

Riley didn't get the chance to answer. Her mother opened the front door. "What are you girls doing out here?"

"We're coming, Mom." Riley stood, sending Beth a 'this conversation is over' glare.

Beth brushed past her with a sad smile and went inside.

But her friend had nailed the real issue. Did Riley believe she was good enough for Shane? Could she make him happy in the long run? Because if she invested any more of her heart into him, she would surely die if he broke it. Better to do the breaking than get broken. Right?

Inside Riley mingled with the guests. The day had gone from sad to heart-wrenching and Riley wanted to curl up in bed and sleep. For a really long time. Of course, she wouldn't. She feared sleep would be a long time in coming when all was said and done.

She said a silent prayer of thanks when the last person left. Finally, she could deal with the emptiness she felt since saying goodbye to Shane. And to the questions Beth raised. No matter how much she'd rather ignore them.

Shane drove through the city lost in thought. Already, the edges of a plan formed in his mind. He needed Nick's help, again. His friend would never deny him, especially this. Nick wanted Beth as much as Shane wanted Riley.

They would have their women. No doubt about it.

He turned into the parking garage of the hotel feeling better. Nick and Katie were probably still playing at the Pier so Shane decided he would make all of the arrangements himself, saving only the most important detail for Nick.

He opened the door to the suite he had rented, surprised to find it occupied. Nick lounged on the couch, his feet on the table, the remote in his hand. Katie sat at the small table near the kitchen area, eating out of a takeout carton. Chinese by the looks of it.

"Hey," Shane said when they looked up.

Katie smiled. "You're back early. How'd it go?"

"Riley kicked me to the curb." Shane threw his keys on the table, almost hitting Nick's foot.

Nick sat up, his feet dropping to the floor.

Katie leapt over the back of the couch and landed next to Nick. "You aren't going to let her go so easily, are you?"

Shane smiled, ruffled Katie's hair and sat on the coffee table, facing his sister and best friend. "No, I'm not. I have a plan."

"What kind of plan?" Nick asked, leaning forward.

"Glad you asked, buddy. We're going to Hawaii just like we planned, only you," Shane fingered Nick in the chest "are responsible for getting Beth and Riley there."

Nick swatted at Shane's hand. "And how am I supposed to do that?"

"I don't know. I haven't worked that out yet. Any suggestions?" Shane fought to hold back his grin.

Nick stood, paced the living area. After several laps, he stopped, stared out the window. "I'll call Beth, invite her to join us and ask that she convince Riley to be her escort. Beth will tell her that they need to get away and give Riley some time to heal, to forget you. And of course, Riley won't know that you will be there."

Even though Shane couldn't see Nick's expression, his body language showed the excitement in his friend. Shane hoped Beth had it as bad for Nick as Nick had it for her. Her buy-in was imperative.

Shane tried not to get his hopes up too high.

Nick pulled out his cell. "Beth, it's Nick. Call me when you have some privacy. I need to talk to you."

"That was awfully threatening," Katie said, throwing a pillow at Nick. "You haven't called her in days and now this? That message sounds like a breakup lead in."

Nick looked shocked. "It did?"

Shane nodded.

"Well, shit. I didn't mean for it to sound like that. I just wanted to talk to her."

Nick reached for his phone, but Shane stilled his hand. "At least she'll be intrigued enough to call. And imagine her surprise when you suggest a tropical vacation."

"Can we go do something?" I can't stand sitting around anymore." Katie went back to her Chinese food.

Shane went into the bedroom to change. He thought of Riley as he stepped into faded jeans, pulled a black t-shirt over his head and then grabbed his hooded Giants sweatshirt, and opened the bedroom door.

Nick gave him the thumbs up, "Can you get her to leave in the next couple of days?" Nick nodded and proceeded to run down the list of flight options.

Shane took that to mean yes.

Nick finished his call. "We're on. Once we have the reservations set, Beth will make theirs," Nick smiled. "She didn't think it was a breakup call, by the way. She figured we would be plotting to get you and Riley back together. I knew I liked this woman for more than her good looks and hot bod."

"Nick!" Katie feigned horror.

Nick laughed. "Beth said Riley's been in her room ever since the guests left. She broke up with you because she thinks she's preventing her future broken heart."

Shane's stomach knotted at idea that Riley broke up with him now because she believed they wouldn't make it. He would prove her wrong.

"Beth gave her hell. Told her you were the best thing that ever happened to her."

Shane grinned. "Beth's right." Now he had to prove it. "Okay." Hope bloomed in his heart like a springtime tulip. "Let's get these reservations made and then we'll go shopping and gear up for our vacation."

"Now you're talking," Katie clapped as she jumped up. She cleared away the remnants of her lunch. "I'll go get ready." She dashed off.

Shane watched the screen as Nick deftly made both airline and room reservations for everyone.

He called Beth back to tell her that the reservations were made. Beth would tell Riley she'd scheduled the trip already so Riley couldn't back down. Nick had booked flights departing from San Francisco International three hours apart, ensuring they wouldn't run into each other at the airport. They would be settled and ready to relax in paradise by the time the ladies arrived.

"You're sure the resort is secluded?" Shane asked. He didn't want Riley to find an easy out when she realized what was really going on.

"Unless she rides off to freedom on a jet ski, she's yours for seven days."

"Good. Let's go shopping."

Nick shut down the laptop. "I'll be right with you. Nick returned wearing jeans and a long sleeved, v neck sweater. A geek through and through, though he could be the deadliest, meanest bastard Shane knew when circumstances called for it.

"Just keep your fingers crossed Riley will listen," Katie said.

"She will." Shane had to believe it.

"Where are we going?" Nick asked as they got into the elevator.

"Let's start at Macy's in the square. We can wait for Hawaii to get bathing suits, but they should have shorts and light weight shirts," Shane answered. "No, wait. Isn't there a Tommy Bahamas' around here?"

Nick nodded. "Good idea."

The mood was light and cheerful as they headed through town. They found most of what they'd need at Tommy Bahamas'. Katie tried on eighty outfits and spent four hundred dollars. Shane didn't mind. He hadn't seen his sister this relaxed and happy for a long time. She still had moments of grief clouding her expression, but mostly she smiled and seemed like the little sister he remembered before tragedy struck.

They went to Macy's for something formal, just in case they wanted to splurge on a nice dinner. Nick and Shane both bought Linen suits in similar colors but Shane chose a hunter green t-shirt to wear beneath his. Nick chose powder blue.

While Katie tried on a sparkly sheath that made Shane's big brother alarm go off, he browsed for a dress for Riley. He knew her size and found the perfect emerald green dress. She'd worn the same color on their first date. It had made Shane's dick hard seeing her in that dress. Of course, almost everything Riley did had that effect on him.

With their purchases tucked away in the trunk, they headed a few blocks away to a cozy Italian Restaurant for dinner.

By the time they got back to their hotel room, Shane was both exhausted and nervous as hell. Beth hadn't called back to confirm Riley's agreement to go. He was going crazy with not knowing when Nick's phone rang.

"Hi," Nick stepped away, just in case the news wasn't what Shane wanted to hear. "That's great."

Relief surged through Shane's blood. He took a breath, then sank down on the couch.

"I'm looking forward to seeing you too," Nick went into the bedroom.

Shane suspected he and Beth were getting reacquainted by the tent rising in his friend's pants as he turned back to close the bedroom door.

Good for him, Shane thought. He pulled his cell from his pocket and called Jake. He would need someone to oversee the gym while in Hawaii. He hired a new manager a few weeks ago but just in case he wanted Jake for a back-up and Jake knew his way around a gym better than anyone.

Chapter Twenty

While her laptop booted up on the kitchen table, Riley made a strong pot of coffee. She'd cried herself to sleep last night and awoke at four in the morning feeling lost and alone. She tried to go back to sleep, but kept thinking about Shane. The idea of going to Hawaii saddened and excited her.

Pacing as the coffee gurgled and popped, Riley ran several story ideas through her mind. She needed to get back to writing and knew some of her experiences and emotions of the last few weeks could be weaved into her story. She knew exactly where to start. The main character in her book wrote relationship columns.

When the coffee settled, she poured a cup, sat down and started typing.

Breaking Up is Hard To Do

No matter whose idea, breaking up sucks. You think that because you do the breaking it should hurt less? Not so much. The bottom line is that you are without the person who made you happy. The one who kept you company at night, made you feel like the most beautiful person on the planet. Made you wonder if what you felt was real. If what you felt would last. But somewhere along the way you decided that the only way to survive would be to cut the person from your life. Like that will change the pain? Hell no. At the end of the day you're left wondering whether saving yourself is worth the agony. What is love anyway? Is love about forgiveness? Acceptance? And when do you really know if it's worth fighting for?

Riley refilled her coffee. She reread the words on her screen and thought they were crap. She'd been writing for two hours.

"You're up early." Beth muttered on her way to the cabinet. She poured much needed coffee into her cup. "I'll be ready for our shopping expedition after I get some java in me."

Riley smiled. "Mornings are the best time to write. Although," Riley began after snapping her laptop closed, "I didn't get anything worth a shit on paper." Riley went to the counter and topped off her own mug. "I'll get showered."

Their flight left at two. Between the last-minute shopping and two-hour advanced check in rule, Beth wanted to arrive as soon as the stores opened.

"I don't know if leaving Mom and Dad right now is the right thing to do." Riley stopped at the door. "Dad broke down yesterday. Finally."

"Riley, your parents want you to go. They said so last night." Beth set her coffee on the table and slid into a chair. "They want to go to Tahoe this weekend and start going through Trevor's things."

Riley joined her friend. Torn between getting away and being here for her family.

"They need to go. They'll feel closer to him in his space."

"I know, but..."

"No buts." Claudia came into the kitchen. "You're going and that's final. Now get out of my kitchen." Pans clanged on the stove. "Breakfast will be ready in fifteen minutes. The two of you have a lot to do."

Riley smiled, despite the sadness she heard in her mother's voice. "Yes ma'am."

After breakfast and a tearful goodbye, Beth dragged Riley on a whirl-wind shopping spree. They ate lunch at the airport while waiting for their boarding call.

Finally they boarded.

"I love first class." Riley cooed, sinking into the wide, plush seat.

"Me too." Beth sighed.

Riley leaned her head back and closed her eyes. She didn't really like to fly but sitting in first class definitely made it easier.

The last three days had been sheer torture. It had taken Beth all of thirty seconds to convince Riley to take this trip. She needed to lose herself in a few trashy beach books and try to forget Shane and the horror of the last week. What better way than a week in Hawaii?

Still, she felt a bit guilty. Her mom thought the sun and surf would be just the medicine Riley needed to mend her broken heart. Riley wondered when her mother had become such an optimist, but decided she liked the cheerful mom better than the somber woman she'd grown up with.

Riley spent the day pushing aside the ideas swimming in her head. The breakup thing hadn't worked for her this morning but she figured out how to transition out of the last scene she'd written and wanted to get her ideas tapped out before they evaporated. She pulled her laptop from the shoulder bag she always carried. Flipping open the machine, she pushed the on button.

Riley plucked at the keys. She finished the transition, ready to start the next chapter. Relieved, she saved her work.

She looked over at Beth, eyes closed, earbuds in. Her friend had been her rock this last week. She knew Beth had been traumatized by Trevor's death but she stayed strong for Riley. Riley also knew that Beth was interested in Nick and yet she hadn't mentioned him in days. Riley felt bad that her breakup with Shane might cause Beth and Nick to back off from what seemed to be a blossoming relationship. But there was nothing to be done about it now.

Riley turned back to the screen, staring at the flashing cursor. Without knowing what she would write, she opened a new document. She felt as empty as the page in front of her. "Penny for your thoughts," Beth said as she leaned over to look at the computer screen. You haven't written anything since take off."

"I have. I finished a chapter. I've been sitting here thinking about writing a letter to Shane." She closed the program. "I can't find any words." Riley shut down her computer and put it back in her bag.

"Maybe because deep down you know breaking up with him is wrong." Beth flagged down a flight attendant and ordered drinks and snacks.

Riley sighed. "Enough, Beth."

"Fine. But..."

Riley glared at her friend. "Let it go."

"Okay, okay." Beth stuck her tongue out at Riley.

Before she could swat her friend, their wine arrived along with a plate of brie, apple slices and soft seeded bread, warm and smelling sinfully delicious.

Between bites they talked about the options for dinner. They were booked at a resort on the big island called Hanekaii. The full-service resort boasted restaurants, spas, pools, golfing, gorgeous beaches with every water sport and activity imaginable.

"How about doing the Luau tonight?" Beth asked. She took another bite of apple, washing it down with her wine.

"That sounds like fun."

They chatted about doing the helicopter over the volcano and the many other things Hawaii had to offer. Riley smeared brie over a slice of bread and took a bite. "God, this is nice." She swallowed with a sigh. "Thanks."

Beth smiled, her eyes lighting up with something resembling mischief. "You're very welcome." She took another sip of wine. "I think this is going to be a life altering trip for us both."

"Life altering?" Riley thought the choice of words odd, but didn't have time to contemplate her friend's' words. The flight attendant stopped to tell them that they were beginning their descent and would need to clean up their dishes in preparation.

She closed her eyes, imagining what it would have been like to share this trip with Shane. Her mind quickly took her in a direction she didn't want to go, so she focused on spending serious girl time with her best friend.

"You know," Beth began, "Nick told me Shane confessed his love for you."

Riley gasped. "Beth."

"I'm just saying. He has it bad, Riley. Why can't you give him a chance? Do you think it hurts less now?"

"Stop." Riley said with little conviction. Her mind had turned down a similar track already.

"Tell me truth, Riley. Do you love him?"

"Yes." Riley didn't hesitate.

"Then I dare you to take a chance on Shane."

The plane touched down on the tarmac and bounced upward, causing Riley's stomach to flip. She grabbed the arms of her seat with white knuckles. Suddenly the idea of a broken heart seemed silly. She thought of Shane while the plane bumped and bounced.

"Oh. My. God. Beth."

Beth placed a hand on top of Riley's. "We're fine." Her friend said as the plane finally settled on the ground.

When Riley gained control of her speeding heart, she whispered. "Maybe you're right."

The plane taxied to the gate. With luggage stowed safely in the trunk of the limo, Riley climbed into the backseat.

She couldn't get Shane out of her mind and she suddenly feared the tropical sunsets and sandy beaches would be intolerable. And call her crazy, but she was actually starting to believe Beth after all. Maybe she and Shane could make it work.

Shane had always treated Riley with the utmost respect. He did nice things for her, always thoughtful and kind. And at the same time, she knew his warrior nature. Knew he could be brutal and lethal. She felt safe with him, even after watching her brother die, when Shane wrapped her in his strong embrace, she felt safe. And cherished. Something she hadn't felt with any other man, especially not her ex.

Beth's cell dinged, shocking Riley out of her review.

Beth looked at the phone, punched a button, then slid it into her purse.

The butterflies in Riley's stomach came to life. "Why didn't you answer?"

"Text message." Beth opened the bar window in the door beside her. "Want a drink?"

Riley needed to rev up her attitude and stop her pity party. "Not yet."

The limo pulled in front of a building surrounded by beautiful plants with colorful flowers reaching for the sky. Riley stepped out of the car and breathed in the luxurious scent of Hawaii. She closed her eyes, again wishing she and Shane could have shared this trip. Wishing she could turn back time and replay the events of the night her brother died. But she couldn't.

The bell hop escorted them to their room, opened the door for them and set their luggage inside. Beth handed him a rolled-up bill. He thanked her and left them to explore their space.

"I'm going to shower." Riley said

"Sounds like a great idea."

Riley claimed one of the massive master suites and unpacked her clothes. She turned on the shower as she put her toiletries away and then climbed beneath the warm spray.

The shower refreshed both her body and her attitude. She wouldn't get caught up in missing Shane and what might have been.

She and Beth would have fun. Starting tonight.

Dressed in a light green sundress with spaghetti straps, a snug bodice and a flowing skirt. Her breasts pushed upward and her nipples hardened against the built-in bra shelf sending a jolt to her pussy.

Thoughts of Shane swarmed her. She hadn't had sex in over a week. And the contact made her hornier than a bachelor at a strip show. She shoved down the desire buzzing in her center and emerged ready to tackle the night ahead.

"When's the Luau start?" Riley asked on her way to the mini bar.

"Six," Beth answered. "I opened a bottle of wine if you want a glass."

Riley opened the small refrigerator door. "I'm thinking something more tropical." She rifled through the contents, settling on a small bottle of coconut rum. She snagged the pineapple and orange juice, conveniently bottled in single serving sizes and made her own version of a tropical drink.

She started with ice in a tall glass, added the entire airline size bottle of rum, added a splash of each juice. She stirred the concoction and took a tentative sip.

"Yum," she said more to herself than to Beth. "This is pretty good. I think rum will be my new favorite."

"Better be careful with that." Beth had seen Riley drink too much on only two occasions. Neither were pleasant. "Don't want you throwing up your dinner tonight."

Riley laughed. "I promise I'll pace myself."

Chapter Twenty-One

Shane showered after his swim. It felt good to burn off the nervous energy his anticipation created but as the six o'clock hour approached, he started to worry.

He dressed in the linen suit and green t-shirt. Taking a final look in the mirror, he ran his hand through his hair which he thought too long. He now had a goatee, shaved closely enough to look like a week old five o'clock shadow on most, but on him it had already filled in nicely and wouldn't cause whisker burn. If Riley let him get that close.

He thought he looked a little *Miami Vice* and wondered if Riley would approve of his new style as he headed into the living room.

"Ooh baby," Katie ogled. "I always thought you were kind of hunky, for a brother and all. But man, you look pretty hot tonight."

Not sure whether to sensor his sister or just say thanks, Shane laughed then decided on the latter. "Thanks, Sis."

Nick walked into the room and Shane waited to see what Katie would say to him.

"Sizzle," was all she could muster.

Nick rolled his eyes, smiling at Katie with affection.

"You guys better get the girl or all of my romantic illusions will be destroyed." Katie hugged Shane. "You look terrific, bro." She turned to Nick, hugging him too. "And, so do you."

Nick ruffled Katie's hair. "Thanks."

"Hey!" she ran to the mirror by the suite's door. "It took me an hour to do my hair."

"An hour?" Shane asked with obvious shock.

"Well, maybe not that long, but still. This humidity makes my hair all frizzy."

"It looks great, Katie," Nick said. "Sorry if I messed it up."

She rechecked her hair, deciding it was okay. After adjusting the dress, Shane thought too tight and revealing, she turned back to them. "You guys ready?"

Shane looked at his watch. Six on the nose. "As I'll ever be."

The Luau was at the edge of the property on a lawn fenced in by waist high plants and flowers. The beach, ten feet below would provide a beautiful sunset.

They chose a table in the back with a clear view of the direction from which Riley and Beth would enter, fashionably late as Nick had suggested. Beth and Riley would be seated in an area that didn't afford them a view of Shane, Nick and Katie. Shane wanted Riley to have a chance to appreciate the view and romance of the night before he approached her.

He turned just in time to watch her sit. His breath caught in his throat at the sight of her. She wore a strapless dress that had her breasts spilling out in invitation. The dress flared at her waist, swishing in tune with her hips. Her hair up in a style that reminded him of sex; all messy around the edges.

Hula dancers provided entertainment as dinner was served. Shane couldn't stand waiting. He picked at his food, only drank half of his Mai Tai and when the party finally began and the couples made their way to the dance floor, Shane's stomach somersaulted.

He felt like a kid at Christmas; a bundle of nerves wound tight in anticipation of what he would find under the tree. Only he knew what he would find when he unwrapped Riley. If she let him.

He came up behind her, his dick responding to her scent. God, he had never reacted to any woman the way he reacted to Riley.

He leaned down and reached for her hand as he whispered in her ear, "May I have this dance?"

She turned so quickly she almost bashed her head into his, but he moved away sweeping her to her feet and up against his chest in one swift move.

"Shane? What are you doing here?" Riley tried to look angry but her eyes sizzled with longing.

"Dancing with you." He smiled and swept her onto the dance floor, pulling her close enough for her to feel his.

The fact that she wasn't wearing a bra and his t-shirt was made of soft silk, allowed him to feel her nipples harden against his chest. He sighed and brushed a gentle kiss over her glossed lips. "I've missed you," he whispered against her neck as he inhaled her scent again.

"I've..." Riley looked into his eyes, then quickly closed hers, not wanting to look at him. He was more handsome than she remembered and her desire for him had her panties damp and nipples hard. "Shane."

He kissed her then as though sensing her warring emotions. His tongue tangled with hers in a sweet, sensual rhythm while they moved in time to the music. His hands slid down her back, cupping her bottom and pulling her firmly against his hard length. She sighed into his kiss and shivered with need.

The music ended and another song began. Although it was faster than the last, Shane continued his sensual dance, revving her body into a frenzy of longing.

"You look good enough to eat." Shane nibbled at her neck and she groaned.

"Shane. Please." Riley wasn't sure what she was begging for.

But Shane knew. He took her hand and led her away from the dance floor. They went down the steps to the beach.

"No. I can't." Riley stopped at the bottom of the stairs. Emotions roiled inside her like a freaking tornado.

"Yes. You can." Shane stared into her eyes with an intensity Riley knew all too well. One she missed with a desperation she now understood.

She lifted a foot and removed one sandal. "Where are we going?" she asked as she removed the other.

Shane took them from her with one hand and grasped her hand firmly in his.

"To paradise." He answered, dragging her down the beach.

He stopped in front of a tropical cottage. "Have a seat right there," he said pointing to the swing. "I'll be right back."

He went inside, returning barefoot, shirtless and wielding two glasses of Champagne. He handed Riley a glass and sat down beside her.

"To paradise," he said as he clinked his glass on hers. His stare bored into her soul and she knew he meant she was his paradise in that instant.

How could she possibly fight this man? He planned for her to come to Hawaii and be swept away and he succeeded without even trying. The second she saw him she melted into a puddle of want and need and longing.

He gently put his arm around her and pulled her closer until there was no space between them. Then, he started the swing rocking ever so slightly.

They sat and watched the sunset in silence. Being with him felt so right that she stopped trying to talk herself into being angry at him. The fear of having her heart broken still loomed in the back of her mind but being with him in this beautiful place, with the smell of tropical flowers all around her and the musky scent of Shane beside her, made her realize that she couldn't not take a dare. She would miss out on so much. She had a week in paradise with Shane and she would enjoy every second of it.

Once her mind was made up, she decided to make Shane work a little bit. After all, he dragged her here without a fight. She grinned, then put on a straight face.

"Oh my God. Beth. I left her by herself." She reached for her sandals.

"Oh no you don't," Shane took her glass and set it on the table beside him. "She's hanging out with Nick and Katie. She's fine."

She stood, intending to make him chase her.

He wrapped an arm around her waist and pulled her hard against his chest. "There is only one place you're going tonight," the hunger in his voice made her clitoris pulse with need.

He backed into the cottage with her still molded against him. She smiled at the flicker of candles and was surprised that she hadn't noticed the flickering light from outside.

Shane stopped in the middle of the room and kissed her deeply with a hunger that both terrified and thrilled her.

He reached behind her and slowly unzipped her dress. It fell free, revealing her breasts with their nipples straining toward him. He groaned at the sight and made a path with his lips down her neck, finally reaching first one and then the other nipple. Drawing each into his mouth, while using his thumb to remind the other of his intentions.

Riley let her head fall back and closed her eyes, reveling in the sensations shooting through her. Her mind tried to intervene with thoughts of how hard it would be to survive losing this man. But she needed to take Beth's dare. Her ex was nothing like Shane. Maybe with him, she could have the real thing and make it through having and raising kids together, growing old together.

She moaned as Shane's hand cupped her damp center, thrusting her hips forward in invitation.

"You are so beautiful when you're aroused," Shane said with that husky, lust filled voice that speared her soul with desire.

She opened her eyes, smiling as he lifted her in his arms and moved deeper into the cottage, toward the open door.

Shane laid her gently on a bed covered with rose petals. Only a few candles lit the bedroom, but as Riley looked around, her heart constricted. Beautiful tropical flowers covered the dresser. Her eyes filled with tears. "Shane..."

He stood above her looking so damned sexy in the candlelight. He reached down and wiped away the moisture sliding down her cheek. "I know I let you down, Riley. I'm so sorry about Trevor, but I've come to realize I'm madly in love with you and I need you to give me a chance to prove that you can count on me."

The tears let loose at his words. Riley didn't know what to say. She loved him too. But she was afraid.

"I know you're scared that I'm going to let you down again, and believe me when I say I can't guarantee that I won't, but I'll try with every breath I take, Riley. I promise I will do my damnedest not to let you down again. Ever." He leaned down and kissed her with a tenderness she'd never before experienced.

She wrapped her arms around him and held on while his kiss grew more intense, more insistent.

His lips never left hers as he finished undressing her. When she was free of her clothing, he explored her neck, behind her ears, down her shoulder to her breasts. He lightly kissed each nipple, then moved down her belly, dropping the lightest of kisses on her stomach.

Riley shivered when he brushed his lips lightly against the inside of her thigh. He blew softly on her center causing her to moan with need. But he didn't stop there. He continued down her thigh to her foot, then worked his way back up her other leg.

Moisture dripped from her aching core.

"Shane?"

He chuckled.

She watched as he dragged his pants and underwear over his hips. He stepped out of them and placed them neatly over a wicker chair. "I'll be right back."

She leaned up on her elbows, watching his nice ass and hard muscles leave the room. Damn, but he looked like a warrior God. Rippling muscles, hard male, tanned skin.

Riley slid up the bed until she reached the silky pillows. She fluffed them behind her, leaned back against the headboard and waited for Shane to return.

He stopped in the doorway with champagne glasses in one hand and a bowl full of strawberries in the other. The look in his eyes told her he planned to draw out her pleasure. She smiled and shivered at the things she imagined he might do to her.

Shane watched Riley from the doorway. He planned to make her beg tonight and from the look on her face, she knew it. He'd have her wound so tight with the need for release by the time he was finished with her, he figured she would say yes when he dropped the M-bomb.

Dirty pool maybe, but he would win her over before the sun came up.

She looked amazing in the candlelight and when she grinned at him, his heart did a cartwheel and his dick bounced with longing.

He walked toward her, staring into her eyes, willing her to know deep down how much he wanted her. He set the bowl down on the table beside her and carefully disengaged the flute stems from his hand, giving her a glass.

She took a sip, swirled the liquid in her mouth and swallowed. Her eyes danced with mischief as she reached for him. His dick hardened more as he realized her intention. She took another sip of her champagne and sucked his cock into her cold mouth. Sensation rocketed through him.

"Oh God, Riley. That feels too good."

She swirled her chilled tongue around the head of his cock, then squeezed the shaft with her hand. He set his glass down and held her head in his hands as she tortured his steel shaft with her mouth. She teased mercilessly, pulling him slowly into her mouth, then releasing him, repeating the motion until he finally took control of her pace and pumped into her mouth. Her grip was gentle at first, then she pulled him fully and so fucking tightly into the back of her throat that he lost it. A vibration more intense than anything he'd ever felt swept through his body as his balls tightened and his semen shot out.

"Yes," he gasped as she sucked every last drop from his throbbing dick. His knees turned to rubber and he grabbed the headboard for support until she finally set him free.

"You. Will. Pay." When his heart rate slowed enough for him to move, he leaned down and kissed her.

He broke their kiss and laughed, grabbing his glass and taking a long sip from the bubbly wine. "Payback time," he said as he knelt on the floor beside the bed. He pulled her legs over the edge, draping them over his shoulders and licked at her drenched pussy. She tasted sweet and musky and his cock sprang back to life as she squirmed under his lapping tongue.

He pushed a finger into her hot, wet channel and marveled at how easily he could feel her muscles tighten around him. He gently worked a second finger inside her as he licked and sucked at her clit.

"Shane, I need you inside me," she begged.

He ignored her and continued his sweet torture. As he felt her body tighten in preparation, he stopped, took another sip of champagne and walked around to the other side of the bed.

She scrambled up and followed him with pleading eyes. He smiled and crawled into bed beside her, pulling her into his arms and kissing her. She shoved her tongue between his lips, sparring with his. When she reached down and wrapped her hand around his hard length, he knew he would be the one to pay if he didn't give her what she wanted.

He rolled them over so she was below him, then kissed his way down her body again until he sucked her pulsing clitoris into his mouth. He worked her into another frenzy of need, and just when he felt her body tightening, he slipped two fingers into her and with his other hand, squeezed her nipple.

She clenched her muscles around his fingers as he licked, then sucked her. She screamed as her body shook in a violent orgasm. He continued to lick her while she trembled with aftershocks until she pushed at his head.

"Please, stop." It was a ragged whisper.

"Oh, no," he said climbing up her body and positioning himself above her. "I'm just getting started."

He entered her hot depth in one long stroke, filling her completely.

"Oh, God." She raised her hips off the bed and shuddered beneath him.

He pulled out and rammed her again, knowing she was about to come again. She met him thrust for thrust and in seconds her walls squeezed around him in another orgasm.

"Shane, I can't..."

He slowed his pace, letting her catch her breath. He kissed her neck where her pulse raced. When it had slowed to a normal rate, he moved inside her. With slow, gentle strokes he brought her back to the edge of orgasm. This time he would come with her.

She held onto his shoulders and stared at him her eyes glazed with passion. "I love you Riley Snow," he whispered as they exploded together. Shane came hard and long, collapsing half on and half off of Riley so he wouldn't smash her.

Tears streamed down her face as she tried to catch her breath. Shane watched her come back to herself, smiling at the intensity of her expression. He understood. He'd felt the same thing. He'd never been religious, but he did believe in God. And something deep and soul connecting had just happened between them.

Riley couldn't open her eyes. Tears spilled from beneath her lids and she felt Shane watching her. Her emotions were tied into knots. She loved this man deep in her soul and she felt some kind of incredibly beautiful bond occur with him when they had climaxed together.

"You okay?" he asked.

She heard the smile in his voice and that was all the encouragement she needed. She wiped the tears from her eyes with the backs of her hands and opened them. Shane's expression darkened.

"I'm good. No, I'm great." Riley's heart flipped over at Shane's grin.

"Me too. That was..."

"Like fireworks on the fourth of July?"

"Better. Mind blowing. Soul searing."

So, he had felt it too. "Soul searing." Riley reached up and touched his face. "I love you, Shane."

He smiled. Big. Then he jumped from the bed and reached behind the vase of flowers. He handed her a Kleenex sized box, wrapped in shimmering green paper with a silver bow on top.

She sat up.

"Open it," he prompted.

The box and lid were wrapped individually, so she only needed to pull the top off. Inside the box was a smaller box wrapped in the same colored paper.

"Marry me, Riley."

She almost dropped the box, her gaze darting to his.

"I know you felt the same blinding bolt of something that I felt. I love you and I want to spend the rest of my life proving to you that you can trust me.

"Oh, Shane." Those dratted tears erupted again and she squeezed her eyes closed. Beth's words echoed in her head. *Take a chance, Riley. You deserve to be happy. And Shane makes you happy. I dare you!*

Riley felt Shane pulling back. She opened her eyes and smiled. "Yes!" His eyes lit up. "I'll marry you."

He took the small box from her and opened it to reveal a gigantic emerald cut diamond set in a simple titanium setting. It was the most beautiful ring Riley had ever seen. Shane reached for her hand and placed the ring on her finger. Somehow it fit perfectly.

He kissed her, then got their champagne. He handed her the glass then wrapped his hand around hers. She leaned in.

"To us. To our happily ever after." The look of total love in his eyes tugged at her heart.

She kissed him gently, then took a sip of the cool liquid.

He set first his glass, then hers on the table and pulled her into his embrace. Her kissed her thoroughly, then made sweet slow love to her.

She woke with Shane's arm around her, her leg thrown over his. Nothing ever felt so right to her than this moment.

"Good morning," he said with a grin.

"Good morning to you."

He leaned over and brushed a kiss over her lips. "How about some breakfast? I'm starved but didn't want to leave you alone in bed to go make something."

"I'm starved too." Riley again felt her heart pull at his thoughtfulness. Being married to Shane was going to be very interesting indeed.

He climbed from the bed and took the uneaten strawberries from the table on her side of the bed.

"Be right back."

Riley got up and went into the bathroom. She took care of business, brushed her teeth with one of the two new brushes on the counter and tried to do something with her wild hair.

She gave up and opened the door to find a tray on the table with a red rose in the center. The only food on the plate was fruit. "That isn't going to be enough, Shane. I really am starved."

He grinned. "I know. It's just an appetizer."

She joined him on the bed. The fruit was delicious but gone in seconds.

"So, what's really to eat?"

"Your choice from the restaurant in the hotel, after we shower."

Nick, Beth and Katie sat on the outside deck at a table with a big pink umbrella. Coffee and juice were already set out when Riley sat down.

Before she could take a drink, Beth grabbed her hand. "What's this?" her friend asked with a huge smile.

"A ring," Riley answered teasingly.

"No duh. Like an engagement ring?"

Riley's smile spread. "Like that, yes."

Whoops and whistles rent the air. Beth hugged her then jumped up and pulled Shane into a hug.

"I knew it!" Katie shouted, joining Beth and hugging her brother with obvious excitement.

Nick wouldn't be left out. He came around the table and slapped Shane on the back, pulling him into a bear hug. "Congrats, buddy."

Shane's gaze found Riley. He winked. "Thanks. Now get out of my way. Wooing my beautiful bride to be was hard work. I'm starving."

Everyone laughed and quickly took their seats.

Shane barely glanced at the menu, before closing it.

Riley did the same, hoping the waitress would hurry as she took a sip of her coffee.

Once the orders were taken, Shane and Nick filled everyone in on how they took down Domino. Katie explained her therapy sessions and the breakthrough that led to her apparent recovery.

"I feel great," Katie said. "I miss Mom and Dad like crazy, and I know they didn't die because of me. But having you and Shane together will feel like I have a family again. I'm so excited." Katie's words were filled with happiness and sincerity. "You are moving in with us, right?"

Riley looked at Shane, then back to Katie. They hadn't gotten past the "yes" and more lovemaking. "I'm not sure what we're doing, Katie." Riley answered carefully, not wanting to disappoint either Katie or Shane. She loved her house and though Shane's was plenty big enough for them, she wasn't sure she wanted to move. "We haven't even set a date."

"Why don't you just get married here?" Katie looked at Shane.

"Katie, we'll let you know what we decide, when we decide it." He reached across the table and patted his sister's hand. "But thanks for being happy for us."

Breakfast arrived. Grateful for the time to think about where they would live, when they'd marry and all of the big decisions that came out of one simple question, Riley dug into her plate of bacon, eggs and crispy hash browns. She seldom ate bacon, but today was a day to celebrate. Right? She loved Shane and wanted to be happy, but she was also scared.

Katie talked about all the events that she had planned for everyone today.

"When did you become the resident tour guide," Shane asked between greedy bites of his pancakes, eggs and a double order of sausage.

"Well, you and Nick left me to my own devices last night, so I figured I'd make good use of the alone time and plan our week."

Shane looked at Nick, who grinned. Beth's face flushed with guilt and pleasure.

"So, what are we doing today?" Riley pushed aside her plate.

"Parasailing."

Riley's stomach flipped. She hated heights.

"Sounds like fun," Beth jumped in, knowing Riley wouldn't hurt Katie's feelings with the truth.

Epilogue

S now fell on the first day of spring, surprising the out of town wedding guests.

The time she and Shane spent together in Hawaii had truly been romantic and magical. They'd worked out a lot of details while in paradise. They decided to live in Shane's house until Katie graduated and left for college, then they would move to Riley's house. Katie agreed to the decision, knowing that she would take over her childhood home when she finished school.

At first Riley let fear overrule all her thoughts and emotions, but Shane's excitement turned her tears of fear to tears of joy. She had seen him in tender moments, like the night in Hawaii after she agreed to marry him. But when he told Katie that he would be signing the house over to her Riley watched her tough guy cry like a baby with his sister. It was as though they were grieving for their parents all over again. In that moment, Riley knew Shane could never let her down.

Nerves flitted like butterflies throughout her body as she prepared to walk down the snowy path carved out by Nick and Beth. The path, overlooking Lake Tahoe and lined in pine branches offered a spectacular backdrop. The crowd gathered along its edges, anxious to get out of the cold. Riley's mother had tried to convince her to move the ceremony inside, but Riley refused. She and Shane chose the first day of spring for the simple reason that it represented new beginnings for them. And they wanted to be married outside with the scents of pine and fresh mountain air swirling around them. The snowflakes adding a peaceful beauty and sparkle to the day.

Beth and Katie waited for the music to start. They looked like ski bunnies in their boots, tights, and fleece vests. Riley dressed in an emerald green pantsuit with sensible black boots. Shane insisted on the color and since Riley didn't care much what she wore, she agreed.

Riley's father joined her under the awning beside the building where they would dine. "He's a good man, Riley. I know you had it tough after Robert, but Shane loves you the way a man should love a woman." Tears welled in her eyes at his words. "Are you ready?" He asked with a smile.

Riley took a deep breath and nodded.

The music started and Katie set off down the path, Beth in step behind her.

Riley looked to her Dad. "Let's do this."

Riley turned the corner searching for Shane's handsome face. The love in his eyes and the smile on his face carried her down the snowy path. He reached for her, grasping her hand as she stepped up onto the small platform provided by the beach side resort.

Her eyes never left Shane's as the minister began the ceremony. She laughed and cried, and when Shane said his vows, icy tears of joy ran down her face. He promised to love and cherish her, but he added his own promise of forever making her shiver with longing and never letting her down.

She loved this man with every particle of her being.

Her vows were much different and her voice shook as she began. "I Riley, take you Shane to be my husband," she stopped and place his hand on her stomach, "and the father of our child."

"Really?" Shane asked his eyes clouded by tears.

Riley nodded.

He pulled her into his arms.

Cheers erupted.

The minister collected himself and continued, "I now pronounce you husband, wife and parents to be. What God has brought together, let no one put asunder."

Also By

Check out these other great books from Michelle Ventura!

Playing With Fire
When Lightning Strikes
Truth or Dare
Dare to Live
Naughty or Nice – a Christmas Novella
Lust

About the Author

Michelle Ventura lives near Lake Tahoe where she is inspired daily by the breathtaking views and fresh mountain air. She wakes early in the morning to go for what she calls her 'sunrise gratitude walks' with her dog Bella. When not working her day job in the medical field, you'll find Michelle snapping scenic pictures, skiing, hiking, or just relaxing by the lake. When she's feeling a bit wild, you'll find her singing at local karaoke venues. Her true passion (aside from wine, food, and chocolate) is writing romantic suspense and fun, sexy, and sometimes super steamy, stories about Alpha males and strong, independent, sassy, females.

You can visit Michelle at
https://michelleventuraauthor.com/

www.ingramcontent.com/pod-product-compliance
Lightning Source LLC
Chambersburg PA
CBHW020629180626
46816CB00003B/884